Winter Goose Publishing
45 Lafayette Road #114
North Hampton, NH 03862

wintergoosepublishing.com
Contact Information: info@wintergoosepublishing.com

I0691044

The Journal of Henry David Tarantula

COPYRIGHT © 2023 by Betsy Orient Bernfeld

Cover Picture by Kathleen Stoll

Cover Design and Formatting by Winter Goose Publishing

ISBN: 978-1-952909-29-0

Published in the United States of America

For W.L. Orient

Praise for *Journal of Henry David Tarantula*:

"Betsy Bernfeld explores the human relationship with nature and wildlife through the lens of several eccentric characters. The narrator is a young biology student and artist whose father is running for mayor. Inconveniently, she has fallen in love with his opponent, Henry David Tarantula, an asthmatic recluse who lives in a cave. And then there is the wolf, who has crossed the border from Mexico and from a previous century. Their story is rich with details about medicinal plants, talkative ravens, jumping cholla, and landscapes of Arizona. Two of the human characters are also wolves at heart, loners more comfortable in the outdoors than with other people. In a surprising twist toward the story's end, another character aligns with the wolf. I was heartbroken to have their story end."
—Marjane Ambler, author of *Yellowstone Has Teeth, a memoir of living year round in the world's first national park*

"In respects an environmental polemic that echoes Thoreau and Abbey, partly a Kingsolver investigation of the human heart, this story presents the desert Southwest in all its modern contradictions. But it's Bernfeld's poetic writing that brings the landscape and its characters fully in view. A caveman philosopher, a fire chief-mayor, and a mother no one dares mess with are seen through the eyes of a young botanist-artist finding her way into adulthood. A resolute black wolf roams through the pages, leaving blood and mystery in its wake. This book will stick with you."
—Dan Neal, former editor of the Casper Star-Tribune

JOURNAL OF HENRY DAVID TARANTULA

By Betsy Bernfeld

Winter Goose
PUBLISHING

This story takes place on the ancestral lands of the Akimel O'odham, Apache, Tohono O'odham, and Yaqui peoples as well as the Jocome and Jano tribes. And before these residents, the mysterious Hohokam and Mogollon cultures.

In humility and gratitude I recognize the original, careful stewards of the rich and beautiful Arizona and New Mexico. Entrapped in my own ancestry of usurpers, I search this common ground for the heartbeat of the land, the wisdom of the Elders, and the love for the Creator.

Prologue

Henry David Tarantula lived in a cave in the desert foothills of the Santa Isabella Mountains, just east and high above the town of William, Arizona. Rocks and ant hills produced lumps in his whorehouse red living room carpet. Fish nets and fluorescent stars dangled from the stalactites above his foam rubber bed. Far to the rear of the cave stood an upright piano with no wooden face to cover its hammer and strings and only a few yellowed ivories scattered across its keyboard.

Henry David Tarantula had silken, spidery hair. He was tall, thin as a saguaro, prickly skin stretched tight across a brittle skeleton. In his dreams he was a white wolf running, running all night. To go faster he ran on his back legs. When his legs tired, he ran on his hands.

I have a picture of Henry David on my bedroom wall, his eyes as dark as the knots in the pine paneling, his wispy hair wavy like the grain of the wood. But despite the picture, and even after all that happened during the election, I sometimes wonder if Henry David Tarantula was ever real.

Chapter 1

HENRY DAVID TARANTULA FOR MAYOR

"Far off something moved at the edge of the earth,
the wind understood and ran."
Tohono O'odham Mockingbird Speech

The August morning that I met Henry David Tarantula held much promise. A single plume of a cloud was painted down the center of the sky like the fine feather of a magic swan. The thin, swirling cirrus, so rare in summer, could have been a lost remnant of the jet stream passing to the north. Or it could mean the desert would get a heavy rain in about three days.

I was wearing my poetry dress from St. Vincent de Paul's, white eyelet lace on top with a thin scalloped calf-length skirt. My mother said it looked like a dresser scarf not a dress. Of course, I carried my notebook. This was a lark. I had pinned my long black braid into a tight knot on the back of my head, and I'd put on my round sunglasses with mirrored lenses painted with pink and blue bubbles as a layer of incognito.

I arrived at Armory Park a little before ten o'clock, entering from Center Street and hesitating at the oleander hedge that ran along the eastern perimeter. I wondered if I had the time wrong. No one was there this Saturday morning except me. Nothing moved except the tassels on the yellow grass. The feather of a cloud had already evaporated. From here, I had a good view of Broadway and most of the park.

Armory Park formed the center of the Town Square, which was the original shopping district of William, Arizona. Over the past five years, however, since the burning of William Hardware Co., the neighborhood had drastically aged. William Hardware was the last of the old downtown stores. With its demise, the heart had gone out of the square. Hardware owner Howard Daugherty boarded up the black hole in the line of shops and allegedly hit the bottle. Shoppers fled to a new mall on the east side of William, and downtown businesses moved up two blocks on Broadway to Congress Street.

Armory Park had once been a gathering place for political campaigning and community fundraising, but it dried up with the rest of the square. The grass was almost always yellow—too dry in the summer, too cold in the winter, the sprinklers didn't work. Beautification projects, once popular among local politicians, were cast aside when some intellectuals won seats on the Town Council and decided that sprinkler systems in town parks should be shut off in order to conserve water. These officials were quickly recalled when they also raised the water rates.

"Progress" candidates, under the leadership of ex-Fire Chief George P. Stone, were the next ones installed. They wanted new industry and they found it in watermelons. A group of Californians calling themselves WM, Inc. had turned 10 acres of desert just south of William into an experimental farm for the purpose of cultivating a new variety of watermelon which, due to a quicker maturation rate, consumed less water. The new mayor and council lowered water rates in town and decimated them for farming operations, though they forgot to turn the park sprinklers back on. As the first crop of watermelons ripened and the election campaign got underway, the incumbents were overwhelmingly popular.

Right at ten o'clock, an ancient panel truck, painted lavender, with THE FLOWER SHOPPE stenciled on the side in florid letters and apparently a muffler problem, boomed down Broadway and into a parking spot outside the Bucket of Beer Bar. Henry David Tarantula jumped out, peeled off a pair of motorcycle goggles, tossed them back onto the front seat, and slammed the door. He opened the rear of the delivery truck and pulled out a sledgehammer and a big sign. Throwing one over each shoulder, his nose and hair both lifted as he caught a blast of air conditioning and stale beer from the Bucket. He crossed Broadway which, even this early in the morning, was a sealed container of hot asphalt and car exhaust. He blew into the park like a metaphysical dust devil.

Henry David headed for the monument in the center of Armory Park, the black marble statue of the cowboy for whom the town was named—either Sheriff Billy Breckenridge or outlaw Curly Bill Brocius, no one knew for sure. The history of William was as addled as the brains of the gold prospectors who told it. But civilization arrived for certain when the townspeople took two significant stabs at respectability. They christened the town William and they changed the name of the Bucket of Blood Saloon to the Bucket of Beer Bar.

In spite of a town ordinance against it, Henry David hammered his sign into the ground. It read HENRY DAVID TARANTULA FOR MAYOR. Dropping the sledge on the lawn, he pulled a batch of papers, letter size and folded vertically, out of his back pocket, fanned them apart and threw them up in the air. With no breeze, they landed pretty much in a pile. Henry David kicked them around a bit. Then he climbed up onto the broad base of the monument, also illegal, and stood under the cowboy's rearing horse, above the names of the World War II veterans (my father was one). Seemingly incognizant of the fact that he had no audience, he began his speech denouncing incumbent Mayor George P. Stone.

"The mayor of this town proposes to outlaw living in caves," he said. "He says it's unsafe and unsanitary." This pronouncement brought on a round of coughing punctuated by a final hawk and spit onto the grass. Yet another violation.

"I am Henry David Tarantula. I live in a cave, and I assure you that it conforms to all the building codes as well as the National Uniform Fire Code. I have enough side yard, front yard and back yard, no unsafe, uninspected plumbing or electrical outlets, and I'm a far distance from any septic tank."

He was wearing the most unusual pants. They were wide wale maroon corduroy bellbottoms, homemade, because the fly looked like it had been chopped out of a pair of Levi 501s and topstitched in.

"So, really, why has the mayor launched such a rabid attack against my choice of housing? Why should he care? Is it because it's located high above him and he doesn't know exactly where? Is it because I don't pay cave rent or cave tax and he feels no one should live without owing someone? He believes all people should be entrapped by the frills and fetters of society?"

Henry David's voice was building. He had the Pennsylvania twang of Jimmy Stewart.

"Is it because it's not progress to live in a cave? It's moving backwards, it's an insult to the builders of houses?"

The sun burning on the desert floor south of William had heated it to critical temperature, and warm air began flowing uphill, north toward the San Miguel Mountains. Midway to the mountains it slammed head on with the boiling updraft created by the asphalt and concrete of William. It careened around buildings and zigzagged into Armory Park. The hot wind whipped through Henry David's fine cloud of hair and flung the top few of his flyers toward Center Street. He raised his fist to the sky shouting, "Go to hell, wind," and that's when he caught sight of me against the hedge. He began ranting in my direction.

"I'm not like all you stupid people who prefer to live in pine boxes. I'm a mutant. A fruit fly in a jar with red eyes." He jumped off the monument and steamed over to the hedge. "You look like a big white flower."

Small white butterflies were fluttering around my shoulders. I waved them off.

"I'm a biologist," I said. "I study flowers."

He got closer than polite distance, peered into my mirrored sunglasses and saw only his own face. He was about four inches taller and four years older than any boy I'd stood that close to. He put two fingers on the nose of the glasses and rudely pulled them off. He didn't scare me.

"I know you," he said. "I've seen your picture in all the political ads." I hated those political ads. "You're Virginia Stone, the mayor's daughter, a snooty debutante. Your chin is smaller than I thought and with a dimple in it." He gave a low laugh but no smile.

"My sister Cynthia is the snooty debutante."

"What are you doing here, Virginia? Spying for your old man?"

"I saw your announcement at the college about this gathering and wanted to hear what you had to say." It was that doggish August period between second summer session and the beginning of fall semester, and I had been pacing around the empty campus looking for any tiny relief from boredom. Empty offices, locked rooms, outdated bulletin boards, his piece of paper in the grass was all I found. I was fascinated by his name.

"So you go to Apache College, do you? Those students are so stupid all I had to do was set up a card table outside the cafeteria and within two hours I had enough signatures on a petition to get my name on the ballot. Geronimo!" He whooped, abusing the sacred college cheer.

I walked over and picked up one of his flyers that had settled nearby. It was a cartoonish drawing of a giant hairy tarantula with a hiking boot on each of its eight legs. Across the top it said STAMP OUT and beneath each heavy boot was one of the following squashed issues:

MAYOR GEORGE P. STONE
THE TOWN COUNCIL
AIR CONDITIONING
THE BUILDING CODES
EXOTIC POLLEN
WATERMELON FARMING

Henry David, once again, began addressing the imaginary crowd.

"I have a simple, eight-legged plan, which I feel will decimate the problems of this town. First of all, I propose to outlaw air conditioning."

Turning pointedly to me, he sneered, "Hah! Is that surprising to someone like you who languishes in the lap of luxury? Tell me you don't live in an air-conditioned home."

"No air conditioning," I said without looking at him. I kept studying the piece of paper.

Back to the crowd. "Those heavy motors humming on everyone's roofs are immoral," he yelled. "Immoral," he repeated to me. "They draw huge amounts of electricity and pour so much heat back into the atmosphere that the average summer temperature on the streets of William has been raised a good five degrees above the surrounding desert. Let them use swamp coolers."

"The swamp cooler," I inserted, still not looking up, "was Arizona's first indigenous manufactured product." I was a walking encyclopedia.

He roared right on. "I say outlaw air conditioning. This, I can promise you, would result in loads of sweat, causing people to flee this town like mindless insects. The desert would be left to the desert creatures."

By now I was getting really angry. It wasn't the air conditioning or the exotic pollen or even his specific animosity toward Daddy.

"What do you have against science?" I struck back mimicking his own tone of voice.

"Science is the work of the devil" was his answer. "The devil. You know—the DEVIL. He's a skinny, spindly creature shaped more or less like a man but with a tail and purple. He has highly placed, pointy ears, tiny horns, a single nostril, and a mustache like a cat."

Was he joking? I tossed his flyer back on the ground.

"Well, it seems your campaign hinges on stamping out various facets of our society. Do you stand for anything positive?"

Henry David bent backwards, looked up at the sky and let the wind roll over his eyes. He raised clenched fists to the blue and shouted, "Water." Then he dropped his head and hands and bowed toward the ground.

I was unmoved. "What do you mean by that?"

His tone softened; his pace slowed. "Underneath this town, down under the heat, the tumbleweeds, the dirt, the sewer pipes, is a cool inner space. Thousands of years of summer rains have filled it, maybe only a few drops at a time, with sweet, delicious water. Unlike the water that thunders down from the Rocky Mountain snow caps, it is water at peace. Silent as a soul. Beautiful as a blue Mexican lagoon."

I dared to let my eyes wander over to William Hardware. Even at this distance, it was like crawling backwards into a nightmare. I had stayed away from the Town Square for five years, ever since the fire. The Hardware sign was now gone, its edifice still blackened. I, too, experienced a dark sense of abandonment just looking at it. When we were little kids, Cynthia and I loved to go into the Hardware. She had always gone to look at Louise Daugherty's crystal dishes, but I stayed with the hardware, opening and closing the tiny drawers of screws and nuts, picking through the barrels of nails while Daddy did business, stealing glances upward at the head of the moose with its drooping beard, the antelope with diamond patterns on its neck, and the three mule deer with huge racks, their enormous quiet more audible than the noise of customers in the store. I thought the eyes were real.

Henry David resumed a more typical tone.

"I am a willow stick," he hollered. "I can't walk these dirty streets without that water pulling on my nose like a magnet. It's absurd that the most obese, water-sucking fruit known to mankind, the watermelon, has been introduced as a crop here. And now the mayor and his troops want to allow the 10-acre experimental farm to become a 100-acre industry. In the name of science, they are sticking down straws as fast as they can and pumping out that sweet water. I hate watermelons."

The wind hit us again, stirring up the papers and the grasshoppers. My skirt flared and floated like a fair-weather cloud.

"So, I guess you're not in favor of turning the sprinklers back on in this park," I said.

"So you're a pretty park enthusiast," he sneered. "You want to usurp some more water, shoot it up in the air, and blow it over the goddamn imported Bermuda grass. You can take your Bermuda grass back to Bermuda. It's non-native. It's an exotic species. I'm allergic to Bermuda grass."

Seemingly to prove his point, Henry David began pounding a fist into the open palm of his other hand. One, two, three hits then "*Ha-choo-y*," he sneezed loudly. "One day soon this town's going to hear a loud gurgle as all those straws suck the last bubbles of water. Then do you know what will happen? No one will lament the loss of a sublime gift of nature. Everyone will be out in the streets screaming that it's their right to drink out of the stinking river."

"You're going to lose," I said.

"I intend to lose."

He turned his back on me, stomped over to the monument to retrieve his sledgehammer, then headed for his truck. I noticed he left his wooden sign behind. He roared down Broadway and it looked to me like he was in the business of selling exotic flowers. After a final glance at the old hardware store, I picked up the flyer I had previously tossed away, stuck it inside my notebook and jotted down *The Flower Shoppe*.

Chapter 2

FIRE
"I'll huff, and I'll puff, and I'll blow your house in."
Joseph Jacobs, *English Fairy Tales*

Five years earlier . . .

All it took was a gas can and a book of matches, and William Hardware Co. one morning at three o'clock shot skyward in a pillar of flames. Luckily, on that particular morning, the owner of the Bucket of Beer Bar two doors down from the Hardware had stayed late to do inventory. On his way out the back he saw the flames in the alleyway. He called 911 at 3:03 a.m.

Almost immediately, the alarm tone went off on the beeper next to the bed of William Volunteer Fire Chief George P. Stone. George, who slept with his socks on and his bright blue International construction truck backed into the carport, hit the floor with his feet at the same time he gave his wife Dot a gentle pat-pat good-bye. His boots were stationed by the wall already inside his bunker pants. Stepping into the boots and pulling up the suspendered pants required less than five seconds. He grabbed the beeper and was halfway down the hall when the dispatcher's voice came over saying, "William firemen report to the firehouse. Structural fire at 30 East Broadway."

George was already in his truck when the address registered. "It's the Hardware," he said aloud as he punched the accelerator.

The Hardware was a 1908 relic. It was tall and narrow with a wooden front, oiled floors and a tin ceiling. It was the only place in town where you could buy No. 8 draft horseshoes, a handle for a scythe, or a 36-inch circular cord wood saw with mandrel and pillow blocks. Howard Daugherty, the owner, still did everything the old-fashioned way, too. He sold screws individually, assembled unassembled toys, repaired items that broke, allowed his customers to charge, and never bought fire insurance. Howard's wife Louise worked right alongside him, a pearl amid the rough setting of a hardware store, and she added a small, surprising inventory of Waterford crystal, English china, and ornate silverware. The Hardware, in the hearts of the locals, was nothing less than a historical monument.

The other old downtown stores had fallen down, blown down and burned down all around the Hardware and were rebuilt in contemporary Southwest style, a little stucco stuck on their pre-fab fronts, a few mission tiles glued to their roofs, and merchandise designed for tourists. But while the new generation of storekeepers had "cheaped" out on their building facades and line of goods, there was no way they could cut corners, chum up to a Commissioner, or in any manner fiddle with the fire code. Not with George P. Stone as Chief of the Volunteer Fire Department.

George was a regular and obnoxious attendant of Town Planning Commission meetings, where he meticulously reviewed commercial building proposals, grabbing every opportunity to beam at news reporters and lecture them on the Uniform Fire Code.

"The only sure way to stop a fire is with a brick wall," he'd say jovially at each session. The Planning Commissioners, quite frankly, hated to see his face. They were sick of the same old condescending brick lecture and accused him of shamelessly promoting his own construction company that, coincidentally, specialized in brick buildings.

"Fellas," he'd retort, "you can huff and puff, but you can't blow down a brick wall." Further, the Commissioners unanimously resented George's popularity with the Town Council. When the Commissioners had proposed a modest $100,000 Town Square beautification project, which included new office furniture for themselves, George had looked into the eyes of the Town Council with his Mediterranean blues and asked for a fire truck. The Council members had ignored the planners and instead voted George a $333,000 aerial ladder truck with an 85-foot elevated platform and water tower that could pump 1500 gallons a minute.

Over the years, with each burning or otherwise demise of a downtown building, sturdy fire walls were erected between each store on the Town Square. And the Chief always managed to get his grinning face in the paper with the quote, "This wall will contain fire." The Hardware, though it had grandfathered its way around the building codes, at least was now protectively surrounded by brick.

George arrived at the fire station four blocks away at 3:05 a.m. Inside the side door he donned his yellow coat and helmet and grabbed his gloves and radio. Jim Lane, who lived only one and a half blocks from the station was already there. George knew because the FIRST LIEUTENANT radio was missing from its hook when he grabbed his own from the peg marked CHIEF. As he ran toward the front of the building, he noticed Lane was on the red phone, a direct line to the Sheriff's Office, and he was writing the Hardware's name and address on the chalkboard.

George hit the buttons for the automatic garage doors, jumped into the Chief's wagon and sped downtown, emergency lights flashing. No need for a siren this time of night. At 3:06 the streets were empty. Not even a derelict at a dumpster. His shiny yellow suit, red flashers and roaring engine were completely out of sync with the slow motion of the night. He sailed past the Hardware in the middle of the block and it was quiet and dark. Maybe it was a false alarm, he thought, or he was dreaming. According to Dot, he often seemed to be chasing fires in his dreams, his arms and legs scrabbling midair like an old hunting dog.

He squealed a left at the Bucket of Beer and slammed to a stop at the alleyway. No, it was real.

"William Fire Base Car 10," George said into his radio.

"Go ahead Ten," Lane's voice replied.

"Back side of William Hardware is fully involved. There's a ten-foot flame showing. Roll Engine 12 and Aerial 16. I want 12 in the alleyway behind the Hardware. Jump the hydrant in front of the Bucket Bar. Put Aerial 16 on Broadway."

One dozen volunteer firemen were already in full turnout on the trucks with the motors running. Engine 12, a Class A Pumper hauling 500 gallons of water, pulled out as the Chief spoke, with Engine 11, the hose truck, right on his bumper and the huge Aerial 16 roaring out behind. Response time was five minutes.

The downtown alleyway behind William Hardware was a tight fit for Engine 12, but it came barreling in from the east end pushing a few garbage cans ahead of its nose, stopping about seventy-five feet short of the fire. The Chief, standing in the alley, gave orders to put two inch-and-a-half lines from the truck's own water supply on the fire immediately, without waiting for the hose truck to tap the hydrant. Flames engulfed a storage shed attached to the back of the Hardware, and George, who had mapped the location of every commercial fire hazard in the county, knew exactly what was stored there. Cases of motor oil, oxygen and acetylene bottles, and about 1,000 pounds of steer manure. While there was nothing in the firefighting manual about that specific combination reaching ignition temperature, George knew for sure it would be loud, colorful, smelly and dangerous.

Standing still during those first moments of firefighting while the firemen pulled the hoses and adrenalin boiled through his own veins was the most difficult part of being Fire Chief. Because George was in charge of the operation, he was virtually eliminated from the action. He had the brains for command but not the personality. He had grown up around the Pennsylvania coal mines, becoming accustomed to the quick relief of tension with a swinging sledgehammer and an enormous vocabulary of expletives. It wasn't much different around Arizona construction sites, and he always had a hammer in his tool belt. But here he stood empty-handed, and not only did the Federal Communications Commission forbid swearing on firefighter radios, Dot never allowed it either. And she was serious.

So, seething inside fifty pounds of fighting paraphernalia with the heat of the fire ricocheting off the walls of the surrounding stores, George quickly reached the jumping point. Up and down the alleyway he bounded. Then, standing right in front of the wall of flames, he threw back his head and howled, "Cheese 'n crackers."

Engine 11, the hose truck, meanwhile had driven around the block and was backing down the alley from the west end also stopping seventy-five feet short of the fire. Two firemen grabbed the ends of two two-and-a-half-inch hoses from the truck and ran them down the alley past the fire to hook into the Engine 12 pump. Once secured, the hose truck driver pulled forward and around the corner laying parallel lines of hose to the hydrant on Broadway. The driver hooked up to the hydrant and by 3:12 six firefighters on four hoses were pumping about a thousand gallons a minute on the rear of the building. The storage shed fire was quickly out, but not before it had crept under the rear door of the hardware store and ignited four aisles of paint. This interior fire would have to be driven back out from the front of the building.

The Aerial 16 crew had parked on Broadway and tapped a second hydrant, laying two two-and-a-half's and one five-inch hose to the pump on the truck. The Chief, radioing from the alleyway, put Captain Bill Corti in charge of a team that would enter the building from the north porch, proceed through the store to the fire, and douse it with two hoses.

Corti was ten years older than Chief Stone but had never sought the command position. He had a thin fringe of black hair greased tight to his scalp, and his barren pate, entire face and neck were baked red from his near 30-year career as a bricklayer in Arizona. For 20 of those years he worked as foreman in George's construction company. Corti had a pronounced beer belly, but it was so tightly corseted with muscle, a flying shovel wouldn't have put a dent in it. He was the perfect second in command for George, off fires and on. He was as calm as a bowling ball and, from long experience, he could translate George's orders as the Chief's articulation disintegrated in the excitement.

"Confabulation visible through the rear window" is how the Chief had put it. "We got paint. Bring in two what-cha-ma-call-its from the front porch and douse the puppy."

"Roger that," Corti replied.

Lieutenants Lane and Robbie Brooks took the nozzles of two hoses. Brooks was small and wiry and a fantastic truck mechanic. Right behind them, manhandling the hoses, were the two biggest firemen, Emery and Rodriguez. On the porch of the store, the men bled the air out of their water lines, turned the nozzles back off and stepped cautiously into the Hardware. Captain Corti followed with a radio.

The path of the firefighters was poorly illuminated by the headlights of the fire truck in the street. The strong beams, though aimed directly into the front windows, were partially obstructed by the bodies of the men, who headed nervously toward their own elongated shadows and an eerie, flickering light in the southern recesses of the long, narrow store. The firemen could sense the rapidly building heat even inside their full suits and self-contained breathing apparatuses.

High on the Hardware walls, more startling than ever in the dim light, were the mounted heads of a huge Canadian moose, a bighorn sheep with full curl, and numerous elk and deer with tremendous racks. These were Howard Daugherty's pride and joy. Even though they had never won him a Boone and Crockett award, they were reminders of younger, more adventurous days. They also had entranced every kid who ever walked into the store for the past thirty years and had even inspired a few biology degrees. Now the dark, looming beasts were omens of destruction. Reflected in their glass eyes, Corti could see the flames at the back of the store.

"Daugherty's gonna hate to lose those heads," Corti said to himself. With each hose taking an aisle, the firefighters passed racks of rakes, shovels and axes and bins of nails, nuts and screws. Then they were into the cast iron pans, coffee pots and glassware. On to flowered china and crystal goblets. To the man, they pressed their elbows to their sides for fear of breaking anything, some remembering their mothers' severe remarks about not touching any of Louise Daugherty's fancy dishes. Rodriguez had said it himself to all five of his children. "Don't you dare touch any of Louise Daugherty's fancy dishes."

It was about halfway through the store that Corti's sixth sense began to nudge him. They were into the plastics. Hoses, buckets and bathmats. Garbage bags, shower curtains and toys. Corti felt a vibration in the air and for an instant he considered that it might be his imagination. But as he looked into the face of a beautiful life-sized doll, her cheeks began to quiver and slide downward.

"Men, retreat. Retreat immediately. Hit the street and stand clear," Corti boomed.

The tentative pace into the Hardware was instantly reversed into an all-out run for the door. As the last two firemen simultaneously leapt from the porch, every pin of merchandise burst into flame and the front windows of the Hardware blew across Broadway.

"We've had a flashover." Corti reported over the radio to the Chief still at the rear of the building. "Everybody's out. Nobody's hurt."

"Son of a bee." The Chief yowled with his radio still on receive. Then flipping it to transmit, he said, "Let's get the roof vent-ter-ilated. Put Emery on top of the porch and have him cut a hole in the front face of the second story. You and Brooks and Lane get on the doom-a-phlage and get a hole in the south part of the roof. I'll get a safety ladder up on this side."

George suspected the fire had already reached the second story office, and there were no windows up there. He not only had to *put* a window up there, but he also had to relieve the enormous pressure inside the building by opening the roof. Right now, any water poured in the front of the building would blow back in their faces.

Emery and Rodriguez teamed up again, putting up a ladder against the porch roof that extended over the sidewalk in front of the store. Emery went up with the entry saw. He was the best man for the job with his tree trunk forearms that could hold the vibrating 30-pound machine at arm's length indefinitely. He would have been an excellent candidate for an officer, but no one dared give him a radio. Swearing heartily, he had a four foot by four foot second story window cut in the face of the Hardware within four minutes. Rodriguez brought up a hose, and the two of them were poised, ready to turn on the water the very instant the hole in the roof was complete.

Corti, Brooks, Lane and two firefighters with a safety hose rode the doom-a-phlage to the level of the Hardware roof. In this case the Chief's "doom-a-phlage" referred to the moveable platform on the aerial truck parked on Broadway. They stepped easily from the platform onto the asphalt shingles and walked the gently sloping roof to its peak. The north side seemed solid, but the south side, below which the fire had begun and where the paint and other flammables were located, was the big worry. With Brooks carrying an electric entry saw and Lane the fire axe, the two men started down the south slope, cautiously testing each footstep. The hose-men stationed themselves a distance back, ready to turn the water on to protect the entry crew. Corti stood right at the peak to get a bird's eye view of the operation.

Ventilating the roof was usually the dirtiest, most dangerous job at a fire, up there in the bad air on a spongy roof with an uncertain amount of structural damage under your feet. Lane and Brooks were fully suited with their breathing apparatuses turned on. The roof was still solid and they quickly began cutting an eight foot by four foot hole near the southernmost edge.

Brooks worked quickly with the entry saw, and Lane, with the skill of someone who had grown up in the woods of Wyoming, axed away the shingles, plywood and insulation within the boundary of Brooks' cut. What the two uncovered was a disappointment. They did not find the ceiling of the upstairs office, but like in so many other old buildings, the leaky roof had been repaired by building a new one over the top. They were now standing on the tin covering of a second roof.

Corti ordered them to keep cutting and relayed the news to the Chief below in the alley and to Emery who, having completed his cut in the front wall, was sitting on the porch roof on Broadway with all the patience of an alarm clock. A precious five minutes later, Brooks and Lane breached the second roof. Only to find a third.

Corti conferred with the Chief briefly on the radio and then ordered Brooks and Lane back to safer ground at the peak of the building while a hose-man ran back to the platform for a rope.

"What's the condition of the roof?" Corti interrogated as the two rested momentarily.

"Still solid as far as I can tell," Lane answered with Brooks agreeing.

"The Chief doesn't want anyone out there anymore without a safety line," Corti said. "He says the fire has had time to move upstairs. Lane, tie into this rope and Brooks, give him a belay over the peak of the roof here. Lane, I want you to go down in the hole if it's not too spongy and give it a few smacks with the axe. We got to get some kind of hole in this roof soon or kiss off the whole building."

Lane, roped up and armed with his fire axe, headed once again down the south slope. The roof still seemed firm beneath his feet, but as he got closer to the hole he could feel the heat increase, and he knew the Chief was right. The fire was into the second story. It was a good two feet down onto the third roof, and Lane would have to stand down in that hole to swing the axe effectively. He decided to ease himself down off the northernmost edge and strike at the southern section, which he thought to be the weaker area. He tamped the third roof with the head of his axe and it seemed sturdy, so he stepped carefully into the hole.

While Emery was spewing obscenities instead of water into the hole on the northern face of the building, George was pacing the alleyway and growling, his eyes glued to the second hand on his watch. The action slowed back behind the Hardware. The Chief still had two hoses spraying the roofs and walls of the surrounding stores to keep them cool and prevent the spread of flames, but the fire walls seemed to be holding. He had set up a 20-foot ladder against the rear of the two-story building as an alternative escape route for the men on the roof. Wedged between the Hardware's storage shed and the adjacent sporting goods store, George had found an empty can that reeked of gasoline. It was arson.

"Shoot the bloody bastard. Hot dog, son of a bee," he yelled, his radio off. Now all he could do was pace. George suddenly stopped walking.

"This is taking too long."

George started up the escape ladder himself. He left the ground muttering a "Hail Mary," but by the time he passed the halfway point, he was shouting in tempo with his boots pounding the rungs, "Holy spirit spit, hot pan son of a bee, cheese 'n crackers, horse feathers peanuts, cheese 'n mother spitting crackers pan, spit, spit, spit."

The Chief poked his head over the top of the building as Lane raised the axe for the first strike. George caught the sickening surprise on Lane's face as the weakened third roof broke out beneath his feet and the fireman went into the building up to his armpits. The safety rope caught him, but it was of no use in dragging him out even with Brooks, Corti and the two hose-men pulling at it. Lane was of no help to himself either, in too deep to get a good grip on the upper roof. He hung like a chicken on a rotisserie.

Chapter 3

THE WOLF
"The wind stirs the willows,
The wind stirs the grasses..."
Paiute Ghost Dance song

Silent as a shadow, the black wolf maneuvered through the trees to the top of the ridge where the den lay hidden beneath a rocky ledge. He carried the hind quarter of a yearling calf easily in his mouth, and his stomach was engorged with fresh meat for the pups.

As the summer progressed, it was becoming more difficult to keep pace with the appetites of the four frolicking furballs. Deer were getting scarce in the Sierra Madre Occidental of Chihuahua, Mexico, and the black wolf and his blond mate had to travel greater and greater distances to elude the ranchers of the foothills who were now on sharp alert for the predators from the dark timber—a menace they thought their fathers had wiped out years ago.

Last night's foray had taken the wolf twenty miles south to an unsuspecting, virgin barnyard and the blazing day was already softening into evening by the time of his return. The den, dug so enthusiastically with his young mate last spring, was no longer so inconspicuous in August, as the entrance was littered with the leg bones, scapulae and skulls of numerous calves and rodents. But the black wolf felt no alarm as he bounded up the hill anticipating a warm welcome, and he smelled no danger, his nose filled as it was with the pungent odor of the meat he carried in his jaws. Even the clouds, little dots of cumulus, spoke of fair weather. He was completely unprepared for the grisly scene that awaited him.

Piled in a heap near the entrance to the den were his four babies, their heads clubbed in and their limbs swollen and frozen in ghastly positions. The wolf let go of his bone and dashed to them, dug his face into the pile searching for warmth, movement, scent, and he vomited the raw meat in his belly. Even amid the overpowering odor of violent death, he detected the sour, salty smell of a human. It sent new alarm through his veins and he looked around frantically for his mate.

Not twenty yards away, on a flat slab of a rock, was a small, bloody mound that he knew had been her. He would have run to her, cleaned her wounds, coaxed her with his nose and buried his head in her luxurious blond fur, but the human had robbed him of any solace. He had taken her head and her coat, and flies were already burrowing into her muscles.

The wolf paced back and forth across the barren rock of the mountainside, whining and whimpering. He walked one direction, then another until night shut down like a trap door.

At daybreak, the wolf slowly descended into the canyon bottom. He walked into the cold creek, faced the current and let the water throb against his chest. The movement of the stream sang to him, bidding him to surrender and flow with it. He laid his chin on the water. It soothed him and he swam and drank. As he climbed out onto the bank, instinctively checking the breeze that wafted up the canyon, he caught the powerful scent of wolf urine. Ears erect, tail high, he trotted down the valley to investigate.

In a grassy opening in the trees, he found a cluster of rocks that reeked with the smell of wolf, skunk and spoiled fish. It stirred his spirits, then his heart froze. There it was again. The rank, salty smell that attended the death of his puppies and the rotting meat of his mate. He launched himself into the air and a heavy steel trap sprang after him.

FROM THE JOURNAL OF HENRY DAVID TARANTULA

I come to this cave because I wish to live deliberately. So that when I am at the end of my life, I will be able to say that I have lived. I want to experience each day so intensely, that when I close my eyes I will still see the desert. I retreat from society's incessant enterprise. I toss out the trappings of society: houses and fashion, institutions and manners, paved roads and regulations. My boundaries become sky, earth, fire, water. I take a new name: Henry David Tarantula. I suck on marrow. I eat grasshoppers.

Chapter 4

THE WALDON
"If a man does not keep pace with his companions, perhaps it is because he hears a different drummer."
Henry David Thoreau, *Walden*

"I think you should go into politics, Virginia," the mayor said. "Take some courses at the college this fall."

It had been five years since my father had plunged off the two-story hardware building into political power in William. He had shattered both heels and fractured one arm in the accident. He had subsequently retired from the Volunteer Fire Department and his commercial construction business, busying himself with local politics, his own small building projects, and avid recycling. His thick, coal black hair was now tinged with gray, and his new muttonchop sideburns were white.

Mom had already left for the office, and Daddy and I were at the kitchen counter. We'd each finished a homemade pecan roll. Mom made twelve pans every three months like clockwork, and now we were nursing our second cups of coffee spiked with a little extra cream and sugar. Mom and Cynthia only drank it black, but Daddy won me over to his court early, at about age three, always saving me his last sip of coffee, syrupy with the settled sugar. I also got his first sip of beer, mostly foam. The pecan rolls were Daddy's favorite and Mom made enough in a batch that he could have one to eat every day. If he wanted to share with me, that was his loss. He always shared.

"Daddy, I'm interested in biological science, not political science." I tightened the sash of my short, light pink cotton bathrobe with white rickrack and my chair gave a little squeak of protest. We sat on tall, ancient kitchen chairs made out of metal and vinyl. If you didn't sit perfectly still, there was a disturbing metal on metal reaction no matter how much WD-40 was sprayed on the joints. Leaning backwards or, worse still, swiveling, was almost a shriek.

"Political science will get you out with people more. Your mother and I think you're spending too much time studying in your room and making all those silly paintings. You need to find yourself a husband like Cynthia. Save the art for when you're an old lady like Grandma Moses."

I gently rocked my chair back and forth a few times, squeaking annoyingly, and traced my finger round and round the pink and gray interlocking boomerangs that patterned the Formica countertop.

"Did you know you have an opponent in the election?" I asked. That was enough to raise his voice a pitch and add a bit of color to his cheeks.

"So they told me at the County Clerk's office. Some weirdo calling himself Henry David Tarantula. Nobody knows a thing about him except, get this, he gave his political party as Anarchist. And he listed his address as 'cave.' Son of a bee." He whipped his chair into a hard left screech and stepped off. "Come ride shotgun for me this morning."

Daddy shuffled out of the kitchen to the den in his stocking feet. I put our two plates and cups in the sink and followed him. He eased himself into an upholstered chair, originally beige, but now the seat and back cushions were greased dark brown by his work clothes. At his right hand was a cardboard box of empty aluminum cans, the family's repository point, and at his left was a metal wastepaper basket for dumping the sand from his work boots at night. He kept those boots under the chair along with a pair of pliers.

"I talked to my biology teacher at the college, and I'd like to get started on a science project before the fall term."

The work boots were tall, coming well over his ankles. They were the kind worn by young men who kissed their wives and babies and breezed off to hard labor each morning, coming home each evening with their boots a little more creased and shapely. But Daddy's boots seemed always new, almost shining. His feet, shaped so unlike feet now, would not drop easily into the supportive, protective cups no matter how far the boots were unlaced and how wide open he spread their tongues.

"I'm interested in the acidity and alkalinity of soils and the relationship of that to the growth of flowers. I want to establish plots in several places around the desert where the alkalinity is high."

Using the massive power of his upper body, which had doubled in size to compensate for his weakened legs, Daddy wrestled his left foot into a boot. The right foot was always more difficult. I gripped the desk behind me for moral support as he grabbed the back of the right boot with the pliers.

"African daisy, a hardy annual, will be the experimental flower."

With a coyote yelp, he forced his archless right clod into its place. The inhuman, frozen metal inside his foot ground against his bones, and even though the surgeon had gone back in, immobilized that joint and cauterized all the nerves, the pain still shot all the way to his head. Tears leaked out of his eyes as he carefully tied the laces.

"How can I help you?" he asked.

"I'm going to need to buy some rain gauges and pH kits."

"Just take what you need out of my recycling money. In the coffee can in the kitchen."

"I want to put one of the plots on the Town Square in Armory Park. Hardly anybody uses that park anymore. I've checked the soil pH and it would be a valuable control in my experiment. I guess I need to get permission from the Town Council."

"No problem there." Gripping the arms of the chair, he raised himself up, balanced, and began a slow circle of the den, tears rolling down his cheeks.

"Don't suppose you could get them to turn the sprinklers back on?" I followed, spotting him as he limped unsteadily, touching the furniture and walls as he went.

"I'll see what I can do."

"I also need to borrow the truck to get to my other plots."

"I don't want you traipsing around out in the desert all by yourself, Virginia."

"Don't worry, Daddy. I was just thinking of putting a plot out by the old Benson place."

"Used to take Old Martha Benson firewood and a bottle of hooch at Christmas."

"I remember, Daddy, I used to go with you. Martha had bristly white hair."

"She was sure one for growing flowers. When Herbert was still around, he put his foot down in it. Said she should concentrate on the cows and grow vegetables if she had any spare time. He died after a few years, of course, and Martha got rid of the cows quick and turned all her plots into flower gardens."

"You used to take me in the back yard to look at the Benson's windmill."

"You named it Squeaky. When the creek and the rain barrel were dry, Martha could always count on that windmill for watering her flowers. She made a good living wholesaling to florists. She always said she grew roses and carnations for cash and sweet peas for love. She even had flowers at

Christmas when we took her the hooch."

He was limbered up now. "Meet you out in the carport in fifteen minutes." He dabbed his eyes and went out the back door whistling. There was nothing in my life worse than riding shotgun.

This time I remembered my headphones. Daddy was already on the Waldon when I came out in a nondescript goldenrod T-shirt and beige shorts plus my bubble sunglasses, though none of these lent any anonymity when sitting on a yellow tractor bedecked with helium balloons and signs bearing a few campaign slogans:

MAYOR GEORGE P. STONE
"P" IS FOR PROGRESS
CLEAN THE CAVES
SAVE YOUR CANS

"Daddy, what do you have against living in a cave? It's not like the cave dwellers are hurting anybody."

"Not hurting anybody? Those cave dwellers are hurting all of society. They've turned up their noses toward every bit of progress that's ever been made. They are directly divergent to the progress platform. Our ancestors came out of the cave thousands of years ago. We've conquered the wilderness. We've killed the big bad wolf. They're a refront to your own grandfather who didn't have shoes during the Depression. They don't produce. They freeload. What do they eat? Where in the world do they take a crap? I mean, go boo boo."

"I know what 'crap' is, Daddy. Did you know that Saint Jerome translated the entire Bible while living in a cave?"

"This joker is no Saint Jerome. More like Fred Flintstone. Abba-dabba-do. And what the H is an Anarchist?"

The tractor wouldn't start. But that was why he kept it parked right next to the bright blue International truck. He got out the jumper cables and soon black diesel smoke was billowing through the carport. I put on my headphones and we headed downtown.

"We can still make rush hour." He had to yell at me over the noise even though I was crammed into the narrow tractor seat beside him. He kicked the Waldon into highway gear and within two blocks had the machine screaming at top speed, 15 miles per hour. I switched on the Rolling Stones.

The Waldon was originally owned by a mining company in Albuquerque. It had power articulated steering and oscillating axles, which made it invaluable on the steep, narrow roads and hairpin turns down into the copper pits. It was just what Daddy needed on construction jobs now that his feet were injured. He claimed he could tiptoe with this tractor.

If it hadn't been so noisy, Daddy probably would have told me the story again about how farking environmentalists had tried to destroy the Waldon one night out at the Albuquerque mine. The vandals had only managed to break the oil and gas gauges and steal the dipstick because the Waldon was such a stubborn son of a bee. The tractor had burned oil after that and the mining company had sold it cheap to Daddy, who had diagnosed the problem immediately: The mechanics had put in a Ford dipstick, which was too short, and they were consequently overloading the engine with oil.

Daddy merged the Waldon in with the downtown traffic, and soon we had a long string of cars lined up behind us, horns honking and everyone looking at us. We blasted in slow motion through the dilapidated Town Square as if there were nothing frightening about the place. Daddy smiled and waved and called out "Vote for Mayor George." Upon receiving a loud and raunchy message from Mick Jagger, I smiled and waved, too. Here came the cops.

A motorcycle cop with his siren on. He was pretty hard to ignore, but Daddy managed for two excruciating blocks until we reached the busiest intersection, Broadway and Congress. There he stopped. Daddy hated cops. It must be unusual for a former fire chief and current mayor, but I think it was a legacy from his Pennsylvania-born, coal mining, union-organizing father. Daddy kept the engine running.

"An anarchist rejects all forms of coercive control and authority." I yelled but Daddy didn't hear me.

"What's the trouble, officer?" he called over the bellowing diesel.

"Get that contraption out of this intersection," the cop said. He was a big white man with a wide face, thin hair, and spaces between his teeth.

"What is it? I'm sorry I can't hear you," Daddy yelled politely.

"Turn the damn thing off."

"Yes sir!" and he turned it off.

"Now get it out of the intersection."

Daddy cranked it a few times, unsuccessfully.

"Can you give me a jump?" he asked the policeman as he waved to his constituents. The policeman, probably a Democrat, slapped him with seven citations, a motorist trapped in the intersection gave the Waldon a jump, and the press arrived with their cameras.

My eyes caught the quick motion of an animal darting out of an alleyway halfway up the block. A raccoon. A rash of raccoons had recently forsaken the foothills, driven out by new subdivisions, and were harassing garbage cans across the town. In hot pursuit of the raccoon was a rolling garbage can lid and a square-headed dog barking like a jackhammer, I discovered upon removing my headphones. As Daddy rammed the tractor into gear and chugged slowly ahead, the raccoon leapt onto the Waldon, first on my lap and then onto Daddy's shoulder, just in time for a front-page photo, Daddy beaming, the raccoon and I looking big-eyed and surprised in black mask and bubbly sunglasses. The dog slammed head on into the bucket of the tractor, tumbling onto Broadway a little denser than before.

"A lot of biology in politics," Daddy commented.

FROM THE JOURNAL OF HENRY DAVID TARANTULA

ECONOMY

What sort of tools and provisions does it take to live in a cave?

A broom. I chase out bats and birds. I am meticulous about sweeping the front porch. I use it symbolically as well, waving it in the air, clearing cobwebs out of my mind.

A sledgehammer for killing scorpions and snakes.

Two aluminum foil pie plates and two tin cups that I hang on the creosote bush outside. They frighten and entertain Clementine, and I can be hospitable to an occasional visitor. Most visitors are giggling girls from the college. Word has gotten out that I live in a cave and they think cavemen must be sexy. I run them off. In Henry David Thoreau's words, "I never found the companion that was more companionable than solitude."

A white gas cookstove.

A truckload of plastic jugs that I fill once a week at night from garden hoses in town.

Fewer and fewer clothes. Henry David Thoreau said, "Beware of all enterprises that require new clothes, and not rather a new wearer of clothes." I found a used, full-length, extra-large Navy pea coat at the Salvation Army store and I am its new wearer. It is heavy and stiff like a full coat of armor. It will protect me all winter from cold, wind and enemies.

Lime. I've dug a latrine about 200 yards uphill and sprinkle it with lime after each use. It has a detachable toilet seat that I hang on the wall of the cave. I ordered the seat out of the Sears catalog, and I use the rest of the catalog for toilet paper. The woman at the Sears Catalog Store in William gave me the Big Book for free and exclaimed, "Enjoy." I enjoy in the open air.

A piece of carpet given to me by Bruce the Snake. I don't trust Bruce the Snake, but the carpet adds a luxurious warmth for sitting. Bruce must have stolen it out of a bordello. It's bright red. The ants get under it and build their hills. I don't disturb them. One day I might eat them.

Food. I drink Mormon tea. I grind mesquite beans on a stone with a stone and make bread cakes or a sweet gruel. I grind jojoba beans into coffee and rub their dark oil into my face and hair. I am becoming the color of the desert. I collect walnuts from Rose Canyon and bring pecans all the way from Tumacacori Mission where the old Spanish groves have gone wild. I pick peaches in Avra Valley and dry them on the front porch. In December, I steal citrus from back yards where it goes to waste. I eat it skin, rind, and all. I keep all these fruits in a line of plastic buckets from the Flower Shoppe in the rear of the cave. I rarely eat meat, but I have taken a few slow doves and quail with a slingshot, and rattlesnakes with a sledgehammer. I roast these on a stick in a campfire in the arroyo.

There is a spring about two miles up Rose Canyon where miners have left a metal tank the size of a bathtub. The stream trickles in filling the tub, and spills out over the top when it's full, the water continuing on down into the canyon. I jump in weekly with a bar of fels naptha. I brush my teeth with a dry toothbrush and chew mint leaves.

"Walden" by Henry David Thoreau is like a Bible to me. I read by Coleman lantern and candle. I have candles perched on every outcropping and indentation of the cave wall so that I read surrounded by fire. I scratch my thoughts on scraps of paper I find everywhere. I stuff them into a large black three-ring notebook. I have textbooks, I bring in library books, I crave music.

Chapter 5

TRAP

"When the crow came for me,
I heard him."
Arapaho Ghost Dance song

It was the rain that saved him. The wolf had fought the trap for two boiling hot days, first in panic and then in rage. He chewed off the metal trigger, and with his free back leg he clawed at the stake pin that held the trap to the ground. He tore ligaments in the right, rear leg that was caught, shredded muscles and nearly severed his Achilles tendon trying to free it. The open wound was filled with dirt and hair. Finally, the pain made him lie down. Thirst made him despair.

The evening of the second day a raven discovered the panting, dirty body. He tentatively set down on the ground a safe distance away. Parading back and forth in front of the wolf's face and then around the entire body, he observed, calculated, then boldly walked across the wolf's back, pecked him on the forehead and quickly flew to a nearby tree.

"Quork, quork," he hollered down at the wolf. The wolf's only response was the slow raising and turning of one ear. The raven settled down on his branch anticipating a full breakfast.

As dusk fell, the wind rose. A black anvil of a thunderstorm, which was gently born in the early morning in the Gulf of California and brought to maturity by the blistering heat of the Sonoran desert, now soared upward toward the Sierra Madres. It broke on the barren ridgetops and hammered the forested western slopes. The rain revived the dehydrated wolf, and it collected around the trap where he had dug, softening the earth and loosening the stake pin.

Chapter 6

DOT

"Dreams are real, as is the light of the stars and moon, and theirs is said to be a dreamy light."
Henry David Thoreau, *Journal, 1857*

"Who-who? Who-who?"
  A mourning dove called outside my window.
  "Who-who? Who-who?"
  August is a perilous place. I was alone in the bedroom in the morning with already too late a start on the day, missing the only time when there was a hope of coolness. My sheets were wrinkled, the swamp box was already humming, the cooler vent above my bed periodically threw out a few grains of sand. All of the flitting larks imagined in May, when it was still mild and summer stretched ahead like a sky blue canvas, had flapped off like buzzards in the August heat. My made-up adventures were as silly as my frilly dresses. There was no substance to my courage. Even the approaching September seemed suddenly dull, school a prison, my legs immovable. Getting out of bed meant nothing would ever be the same again, like after fire sirens, or like when Cynthia announced her engagement. So I lay in my sweaty linens reliving the free fall from the Hardware roof, hearing again Daddy's drugged muttering from the hospital bed, "Don't die, don't die."
  "Who-who? Who-who?" The pulsing question repeated.
  "Cha-tah'-qua," responded a Gambel's quail.
  The sun was already blaring through the closed curtains and I studied the grain in the pine-paneled walls of my room. There were blond sunbursts and long vertical ladders. One dark section must have come from below the ground as it was riddled with mud brown circles where roots had sprouted out of the trunk. I searched for pictures in the knots and lines of the wood, the violent patterns like the sound waves of some music I couldn't read. I wanted something so much, but I didn't know what it was. My ceiling was cerulean blue.
  Mom stuck her head in the door at 7:45.
  "You're being lazy, Virginia."

Mom never looked up. She didn't know that I had painted my white ceiling blue. I did it in July when it was too hot to be outside. I went to summer school classes in the morning, but in the afternoon I was closed up in the house, locked up in my room. The swamp cooler with its squeaky hum and damp air was my vague, whispering companion. I took a can of glaze and added a dollop of cerulean blue—deep azure, just a hint of green—that Michelangelo used on ceiling of the Sistine Chapel. I rolled it on in one afternoon, left my windows open, the cooler on, my door closed. The odor went unnoticed. The glaze made the color translucent. It was like looking at the clear blue sky.

I still didn't get out of bed. Summer school was over. I didn't even want a cup of sweet coffee with my dad. I waited until both parents had left for work and the white heat of the day set in. Finally, I dragged myself dizzily out to the back yard still in my shortie pajamas, bright magenta with three layers of ruffles across the chest and two around the bottom of the shorts. Cloud report: None. I gave up hope on the feathery cirrus of three days ago. There would be no rain today. I didn't wash my face or redo my disheveled braid. I got out my paints and a ladder from Daddy's workshop and hauled them back into my bedroom. If I couldn't see clouds, I'd make clouds.

For the first layer, I mixed half blue, half white plus a measure of glaze so the colors wouldn't be too opaque. Using one of Daddy's holey undershirts from the rag bag in the linen closet, I dabbed clouds onto the cerulean ceiling of my bedroom. I would add more layers of paint later, progressing through mixtures with less blue, whiter, to finally pure white, building cumulus, waiting for rain. The monsoons were late this year. We could usually count on rain by the fourth of July, but it was already after the first of August and we'd had none. The storms were staying south in Mexico. In the end I would bring in some yellow and pink, changing from a cotton rag to a sponge for a different texture, trying to capture sunrise.

My mother drove me to it.

"Get your head out of the clouds, Virginia" was her favorite expression.

Mom and I were sitting in the kitchen when Fire Captain Bill Corti walked timidly up the sidewalk at six o'clock in the morning that August day five years ago, Daddy's slashed fire boots under his arm. I saw the youth drain from Mom's face.

"He's okay," Captain Corti had said. "He fell off a roof. He's hurt his feet and we've taken him to St. Joseph's." Perspiration leaked down his forehead and his voice shook. Mom didn't move, didn't respond. Captain Corti filled in the horrifying gap of silence with a jabbering report just about as inarticulate as my father would have done. "He saved Lieutenant Lane. Pulled him out of a hole, then the whole roof collapsed. We had Lane on belay but George, well George, went the other way. He was running through mid-air then I couldn't see him and I had to make the final call, 'surround and drown.' We used the aerial platform. Fifteen hundred gallons per minute. The Hardware is gone and Broadway is running like a black river. The firewalls held."

"Today is his birthday" was all Mom said.

When we walked into the emergency room, we could hear Daddy calling for her, hollering away, not even knowing where she was or when she'd be there.

"Dot...Dot...Dot..."

He was packed in ice from the knees down waiting for surgery. We saw him for only a moment and then the nurses wheeled him away.

Mom and I sat in the waiting room of the surgical wing. She stared into the pages of a *Good Housekeeping* magazine, but she never turned them. She didn't say a word. After about an hour I went downstairs to the gift shop. All they had were sickening little pink bouquets properly arranged and I couldn't afford them. For once in my life I knew exactly what I wanted. I ran out the front doors of the hospital, across the acre parking lot and out onto Fifth Street.

The traffic was heavy and I was afraid to cross to the shopping mall on the other side of the street. I couldn't see clearly, and my face was streaked with tears. I turned right and ran three blocks to Lucky's Grocery. They had a whole table of potted chrysanthemums and I picked out some yellow ones. Only $1.89. No perfume, just bright color. I walked back to the hospital cradling them like a tiny child even though they were protectively wrapped in cellophane.

"Don't be silly, Virginia," Mom said when I got back, but I sat there in the waiting room anyway with the potted flowers on my lap.

About two o'clock in the afternoon we saw the doctor pass by in the hallway. Mom dropped her magazine on the floor and chased after him. I could hear her hard heels pounding down the shiny linoleum. I put *Good Housekeeping* back on the table and stood in the doorway with my flowers.

A nurse came by and I sort of croaked, "These are for my father."

That seemed to be enough, because she smiled and carefully took the chrysanthemums.

"I'll make sure they get in his room."

"Daddy's out of surgery," Mom said when she came back to the waiting area. "The doctor said he came through just fine, he's in the recovery room, and we should get something to eat. That's all I could get out of him."

"I always carry a peanut butter and jelly sandwich in my backpack."

For once Mom didn't make a comment about me dragging my pack everywhere instead of carrying a purse. My science kit wouldn't fit into a purse. We sat together on the cold turquoise Naugahyde couch in the waiting room—Mom refused to go downstairs to the cafeteria—and split the sandwich.

"This is the best peanut butter and jelly I've ever had," Mom said.

She gave me some change and asked me to go find a machine and buy us both a Coke.

When I came back, Cynthia and her boyfriend Everett were there. They had driven in from Tucson where they were going to the University. Cynthia and Mom were sobbing in each other's arms. I didn't know why Cynthia had to bring her dumb boyfriend. He was always hanging around as if he were part of the family.

After they settled Daddy into his regular room, we all got to go in and visit him for a minute even though he was still asleep. My little pot of yellow flowers was on a table next to his bed, dwarfed by a huge formal bouquet from the firefighters. Everett drove Cynthia and me home, and Mom stayed on at the hospital.

Mom, for a time, put on blue jeans, tied her golden hair on top of her head in a ponytail and drove Daddy from fire to fire in her station wagon. He sprawled across the back seat, both of his legs and one arm in casts, his wheelchair squeezed in with him. Mom must have driven with her left arm hanging out the window, because that one arm became as tan as Daddy.

"Forget your dreams, Virginia." Another one of Mom's favorites.

Once, in the back of the car, Daddy let a swear word slip out. Mom said next time she'd take him and his wheelchair to the County Courthouse, plant him at the top of the handicap ramp entry on First Street, and send him barreling down into traffic. But otherwise, she endured Daddy's constant insults to her driving, his head sticking out the window to advise other motorists, and his frustrating attempts to fight fires from the back seat. She lasted until the casts were off, physical therapy was tried and abandoned, and Daddy was wildly and painfully limping around on his own. Then she went downtown and got herself an office job.

"Cynthia's getting married and Virginia's in high school," she said. "It's time I went back to work."

Mom made cameo appearances during Daddy's political campaigns and the family paperwork still got out on time, but every morning at 7:45 she clacked off in her high heels leaving silence and dust hovering in all the corners.

Daddy still came into the house during the day yelling "Dot...Dot...Dot..." always checking the bedroom to see if she might be there. He did even the simplest chores—bandaging a finger, fixing a sandwich—with stubborn ineptitude until 5:15 each evening when Mom returned and the house suddenly seemed organized again.

"You need to get out of the house more, Virginia." This was last night's conversation. "Why don't you find yourself a nice boyfriend. Cynthia met Everett in high school."

"Mom, I don't want to meet Everett."

"Don't get smart with me. You're starting your second year of college and you've hardly been out on a date. You even skipped your Senior Prom. You're such a bookworm. You can't stay around here and be Daddy's girl all your life."

"I can't help it if guys don't ask me out."

"Try smiling more."

I added a stab of gray to my first layer of clouds.

FROM THE JOURNAL OF HENRY DAVID TARANTULA

CLEMENTINE

She bites me on the ear, she bites me on the butt, she watches me in the window as I sleep, she has stolen my spoons, my underwear, my money. She struts on my porch flicking her shiny feathers. She coos (more like quorks) when I play Clementine on the harmonica. She's a parody of the sexuality of nature. A caricature of loneliness seeking fulfillment. I do not need love or companionship. I run her off with my broom.

extreme northeast corner of sky, there is a clump of mackerels like a gray layer
of fat on cold soup. I sprinkled on 3.0 liters of William tap water.

My technique was incredibly primitive. I measured soil pH to the nearest whole number with litmus paper. I dipped the paper into a solution of the soil and distilled water and compared the color to a chart that came with the pH kit. I had no electric, digital pH meter and neither did Apache College. I determined the growth of flowers by lying on my stomach trying to hold curling stems steady against the metric side of a six-inch plastic ruler that came in a Christmas card from William Hardware years ago. I took soil samples, but I had no way to perform a chemical analysis of them. Under the microscope, I took a closer and closer look, but felt myself straying further and further from meaning.

Up at the cave, the raven strutted in the limited space of the window, almost marching in place, incessantly smacking her lips. Her remarks took on a metallic mix of sounds.

"Thunk thunk ding, thunk thunk pop, squeak squeak snap. Hiccup."

A tennis shoe came flying out the window, and the raven retreated.

She was a vision of female rejection as she paced the desert floor outside the cave, murmuring, tail drooping, head tousled, cape askew. But soon she couldn't resist a look at the shoe. She flew into a creosote and viewed it from there. No movement. Setting down a safe distance away, she espied it with both eyes. She darted around it, not getting any closer. She circled it in the air, watched it again from the bush, again from the ground. She trilled twenty times, then gurgled.

It was the dangling shoelace that seemed to accelerate her decision making. She danced up to it and back. By the time Henry David staggered stiffly out of the cave, wearing nothing but his hand over his eyes against the sun, she had removed the lace, flown away, and was probably rapturously weaving it into a nest.

I flew away as well.

The following Wednesday I was back at the plot with my instruments. Henry David crawled out from behind a rock.

"What are you doing in my yard?"

"This is not *your* yard. This land belongs to the Forest Service."

"Well, I have squatter's rights on it."

"Squatter's rights no longer stand up in court. Besides, I'm not going to bother you. I'm merely conducting a science project. The soil here has an extreme alkalinity due to its geologic history and limestone source material, and it is a valuable asset to my experiment. I'll be very quiet and careful not to bother you."

"What are you planting anyway?"

"African daisies, a hardy annual."

That set him off. "Flowers. Exotic pollen. How do you know I'm not allergic to that? Not going to bother me, huh? What about my nose?"

"Don't get excited. Hardly anyone is allergic to African daisies. They're pollinated by butterflies. It's the wind-pollinated plants like triangle leaf bursage and canyon ragweed that cause hay fever. But if daisy pollen does irritate you, I'll be glad to dig them up."

"The least you can do is plant something I can eat."

The next Sunday I arrived at 8 a.m. with my watering can and a bag of bulbs in the back of the blue International. Henry David was roosting in his front yard. The raven sat silently in the upper branches of the pecan tree, facing east, eyes closed, shoulders hunched. On the other side of the pecan tree from my daisy plot, so as not to contaminate the experiment, I dug a half dozen small holes with a hand trowel and inserted the bulbs. There was one tiny puff of a cloud to the southeast.

"What are you planting now? More flowers?"

"Nope. I'm planting something you can eat."

"Oh really, what?"

"Garlic."

Henry David reached back into the knife sheathe that he wore on his belt and pulled out his harmonica. He tapped it on his open palm, hummed a few bars and began playing. The harmonica wheezed as he sucked and spit into it, and Henry David began rocking and slapping his leg to some incomprehensible tune.

Cause and effect is mathematically impossible to prove, according to my statistics instructor at Apache. Though they tend to speak as if they are positive, scientists must be content with correlation, that is, one variable is related to another, and they must allow for random error. In my notebook I recorded all of the inadequacies of my experiment, yet still I set my standards high: alpha=.01. In other words, I would concede that alkalinity has influenced the growth of my African daisies, thus rejecting the null hypothesis, only if I were 99% mathematically sure.

FROM THE JOURNAL OF HENRY DAVID TARANTULA

GRASSHOPPER

In the early morning when it was still stiff, I caught a grasshopper in my empty water bottle. I set the bottle on a rock in the sunshine and lit a pipeful. As the sun warmed the bottle, the grasshopper became more agitated. As I smoked, he also got bigger. I held the bottle to my face and we looked eye to eye. I wished I had chosen a smaller one for my first. I took the top off the bottle, shook the insect into my hand, and slammed him into my mouth head first. He became even more agitated. He railed from cheek to cheek, crackling hot, kicking with six legs although the sixth was hanging out of my mouth. I rolled on the ground, fighting the air with my own arms and legs, screaming out of my nose. He bit me on the roof of my mouth and the back of the tongue, inciting my gag reflex, though I kept my lips tightly sealed. Finally, I crunched down. He made one last swab of my tonsils with his antennae and was quiet. I lay quietly, too, and began to taste him. First there was a drab vegetable taste, like eating a dusty leaf. Then the slight flavor of salt leaked out from between my clamped teeth. A little later, a shot of bitterness penetrated my salivary glands, burned into my nasal passages and eye sockets, causing all to release a rush of water. I swallowed him almost whole.

Chapter 8

SEÑOR RAVEN

"When I would re-create myself, I seek the darkest wood, the thickest and most interminable...out of such wilderness comes the Reformer eating locusts and wild honey."
Henry David Thoreau, *"Walking"*

The Mexican child climbed over the low fence into the chicken yard to spread some feed and collect the morning eggs. She spotted the evidence of the previous night's debacle and ran wailing back to the house.

"*Mama, Papa, Trampa esta aqui.*"

Papa grabbed his gun and ran out to the chickens. No chickens. Feathers, a few clean-picked bones. The tracks in the soft dry dirt were plain. There were large prints of a wolf who seemed to be dragging a trap and a chain on his right hind leg. Criss-crossing the murder scene were the three-toed tracks of a large bird.

"*Si,*" Papa said. "*Y Señor Grajo estaba aqui tambien.*"

It had been a month since the black wolf had slunk into the dark timber dragging the bloody ten-pound trap with him. All August long he had fought the trap, the sky a simple palette of cerulean blue. For the first week he could do little more than lie on the forest floor. He licked his wounded leg and the surface tears healed quickly. But the inner damage to his muscles and ligaments caused his lower leg to dangle uselessly, and the metal trap against his bones caused a pain that would not go away.

The wolf chewed relentlessly on the trap and managed to bite off the spring, but the steel jaws and chain remained intact. He filled his stomach with what was close by, mostly grass and twigs, moths and worms, and he used his powerful teeth to daintily pluck tiny ripening huckleberries. The black hair on his chin began to show white, though the wolf was only three years old.

The raven, who had long ago given up the thought of wolf eyeballs for breakfast, still visited the wolf frequently and seemed amused by his predicament. He flew around the wolf's head, "*Quork, quork,*" and strutted in front of his face, just out of the injured animal's sluggish reach. When ignored, the pesky bird would peck at the wolf's tail until the wolf acknowledged his presence with a snap of his jaws.

The wolf had also given up the idea of a raven brunch, and one evening when his hunger became more intolerable than his right leg, he slowly headed up the ridge. Inch by painful inch, the wolf dragged the trap, and each time the awkward metal contraption snagged on a rock or bush, a jolt of lightning surged up his leg and spine leaving him sweating and panting in the grass. The wolf soon discovered that by flexing his right thigh, he could hold the trap away from the ground and he proceeded up the hill on three legs. But his legs were weak, and he rested often.

At dawn the wolf lay at the top of the ridge. He could see down the draw where the creek ran, and the grassy openings where deer ventured to feed in the early morning. To the south and east were more ridges and dark forested slopes, the wilderness in which he had been born. The north was unknown to him and westward lay the gentle foothills that crawled with the slovenly barnyards and acrid presence of humans. He caught a movement in a meadow near the creek. It was a doe going for a drink. He would have slipped off the ridge, faded noiselessly through the trees and taken her easily. Except for the trap. He now did not have the strength or speed to kill a deer. Or even a skunk. The realization seeped into his brain, and he rested his chin on a rock. The rising sun began to warm his dark coat and he fell asleep.

Trap was awakened when the raven fell out of a high climb and swooped past, inches away from his face. Ordinarily, the wolf would have pretended not to notice, but this time Trap smelled meat in the raven's beak. He was quickly alert and saw the raven land on a nearby boulder. The raven had a flat strip of meat, which he smugly held under one foot and consumed with exaggerated pecking motions. The wolf, tucking the trap close to his body, limped toward the raven on three legs. His nose told him the meat was highly spiced and most certainly came from a ranch in the foothills. He pretended interest in a butterfly and stooped for a drink from a pothole in the rock, all the while edging toward the raven. As the wolf came within reach, the raven, with an insulting squawk, shot upward with the meat and then dropped the small piece that was left on the wolf's head.

"Trill trill thunk gong."

The wolf caught it on the rebound and swallowed it without even tasting it. In spite of his dread, he had to acknowledge that his livelihood could only be made in the foothills.

It wasn't hard for Trap to find the source of the spicy meat. After all, he was following a raucous raven in the broad daylight. But just how to get a meal for himself might be a more difficult problem. In the back yard of a rather dilapidated farmhouse stood two large wooden drying racks draped with onions, chili peppers and spicy strips of venison. The yard was meagerly fenced with posts and poles, not even enough to keep the deer out of the garden, let alone to hinder a hungry wolf who was coming in on his belly.

Trap stopped just inside the fence in the cool, damp well of a pomegranate tree. Though it was late afternoon, he knew he must wait until night to be safe. He rolled over on his back and ate a pomegranate. The raven, to the wolf's horror, flew onto the roof of the farmhouse and began tapping loudly on the metal stovepipe. Out the back door came the farmer's wife, who grabbed the broom on the porch. The wolf flattened himself in the mud, hardly able to breathe. The conversation in Spanish was clearly understood.

"Manuel," she called back toward the house, "that bird is back. I told you to stay out here and watch for him. He's already stolen part of our jerky." She began beating on the edge of the roof with the broom. "Get out of here. Shoo."

"*Ka ka ka ka.*"

"Calm down, *cariño,*" said Manuel as he strolled out of the house. "It is too hot for me to stay outside all day. He has only taken a few pieces. It will soon be night and he will go to sleep and the meat will be safe."

"Of course, it will be safe. You are taking the racks inside right now. The coyotes could come at night and now Hortensia is saying there are wolves."

"Hortensia has a wild imagination. There haven't been any wolves in these mountains for thirty years."

"Manuel, Hortensia saw the skin that Juan Moreno took four weeks ago just up in Slate Creek. It was no coyote. And Juan said he set a trap for the bitch's mate and the animal was so big he ripped the trap right out of the ground."

"I'm taking the racks inside, *cariño*. But believe me, there are no wolves in these mountains." Manuel picked up one of the racks and headed for the house and his wife walked ahead of him holding the door.

The wolf watched in desperation as part of his dinner disappeared, and hunger and fear knotted together in his stomach. He gathered the trap to him and on three legs he quickly covered the remaining length of the yard. He gobbled meat from the remaining rack without chewing and had emptied most of it before the farmer emerged from the house. He kept eating as the farmer stopped still in surprise.

"Mama, quick, my gun."

He still ate as the farmer ran into the house, and he took one last grab at the rack as the farmer flew back outside. As he bolted for the woods, the wolf crunched down on a mouthful of jalapeños. He charged through the fence, caught his trap on the lowest pole and slammed face down in the dirt. The fall knocked the wind and the jalapeños out of him and sent screams of pain up his leg and back.

Trap slowly picked himself up. The farmer, shaking like a nervous grasshopper, finally got his bead on him. But as he started to squeeze the trigger, he found he was staring into the beady eyes of a raven. The raven shrieked, the farmer shrieked, the gun went off high in the air, and the wolf got away.

BIRD

Bird is what my father called me. He eats like a bird, he's scrawny like a bird, he squawks. Even as a small child, I knew he was mocking me. I'd awaken to his dark presence in the hospital room, and he would leave, not saying anything. My father is a big man, a football player in his day, a captain in the army. His son a bird. My mother thought it was cute to be a bird and she called me Tweetie. My mother covered with bangles, lipstick and perfume. Jingling. Jabbering. A noisy flitting presence. It was hard to breathe with her perfume in the air.

Chapter 9

CLEMENTINE
"Four times he bends upward and talks
Jumps up and down and talks"
Tohono O'odham Mockingbird Speech

One morning I took my art supplies up to Henry David's cave. After tending my science project, I set up my easel under the pecan tree. I painted last night's dream. There was a lone, renegade cloud with permanent zigzagging lightning bolts hanging beneath it. It had raced around the valley, its magnetism jerking trains off their tracks and semi-trucks into the air. I made the cloud impenetrable black. On the lightning I tried out some new fluorescent lime green paint. The airborne vehicles and the silhouette of a mountainous landscape were deep purple.

I knew Henry David was watching, though I couldn't see him anywhere. It was a sensation in my hair and on the back of my neck. He was behind me. It made me clumsy, then irritated. I added some fluorescent pink lightning bolts that weren't even in the dream.

When he did pop up, he was above me, calling down from the direction of the cave, inviting me for a cup of tea. As I came up over the hill, a camp stove was whirring away on his limestone porch, and steam started pouring out from under the rattling lid of a cookpot. Henry David turned off the stove, added a handful of leaves and stems to the pot of water, and sat back to let it steep. The silence was startling without the noisy stove.

"What kind of tea is it?" I asked.

"It's medicinal. Whitethorn acacia to settle my stomach and a few stems of Mormon tea for my asthma."

I sat down on the limestone. Henry David wore a pair of tattered cut-offs with an inch of fringe around his thighs where the legs had unraveled. No shirt. His nose and chest were whistling. He served the tea in aluminum Sierra cups, very hot on the lips. The tea tasted like dirt, but I felt a slight lift in my chest.

"How long have you lived up here in this cave?"

"One year, almost to the day."

A large raven stood like a sentry on top of the saguaro by the front door. She was motionless yet ruffled as if she had just been through a battle. As we sipped the tea, she began to preen. She pulled feathers through her beak making the sound of crumpling paper.

"I was wondering if you would put a painting on my living room wall," Henry David said.

"*Phht, phht, phht,*" came from the saguaro. The raven was starting to remind me of my mother.

"I have paint," he said.

The raven flew down to the window of the cave. It wasn't like I was going to be without a chaperone, and it was a good excuse to forsake the tea. I followed Henry David into the cave.

The single chamber was dimly lit by the natural light of the doorway and the one trapezoidal window, now partially blocked by the big black bird. My skin contracted in the clammy cool air, and as my eyes became accustomed to the gray light, they were drawn upward to drapes of fishnets that lowered the high ceiling and an army of glow-in-the-dark paper stars that dangled beneath them. The uneven floor was partially covered with a reddish, lumpy piece of carpet and was strewn with books. All the way to the back of the cave was the only furniture—an upright piano, also piled with books.

Henry David sat down on a round, claw-legged piano stool and began plinking at the keys. As I approached, I could see that the instrument was more like the skeleton of a piano. The wooden panel that forms the front of an upright was missing, the strings and hammers revealed. Only a few ivories remained on the keyboard like several yellowed teeth in an ancient skull. Henry David was playing on the boney stubs of the key supports.

"There's paint over there in the corner." I followed the general direction of his pointing finger. The corner was filled with a tall pyramid of slightly scrunched empty aluminum cans, and it smelled like the alley behind the Bucket of Beer. There was also one can of yellow automotive paint.

"Anything besides yellow?"

"Nope. I got busted for writing political comments on a bulldozer, and the judge made me touch up the paint."

There was one more irreconcilable difference between Henry David and my father. Defacing a yellow tractor. I found a bucket containing a brush and a paint stick, which I used to pry open the can and give it a stir. There wasn't much I could do with yellow.

"Which wall?"

"Any which one."

Henry David began swaying. He stretched backwards, eyes closed, nose up, and hit the keys with curved fingers, then lifted his hands high for the next pounce. I started near the piano, painting a large yellow ball, the sun. Henry David's hands seemed to be in the wrong place on the keyboard. There was no melody, as if he were groping for something but didn't know what it was. I made sun rays that crept around the piano and the music picked up in pace and volume. The notes were at war with each other. They banged off the walls, the bird exited the window sill, and my yellow sunbeams wove all over the room.

Suddenly, perhaps it was the paint fumes, Henry David stopped abruptly and walked out of the cave. I threw down my messy brush and followed him. He turned on me.

"Your science project is a fake, isn't it?"

The raven was back on the saguaro.

"Of course it's not a fake."

"Well, what's the point of flowers?" It was as if an elf had walked up his cheeks, a bucket of brown paint in one hand, dark green in the other, and dumped them in his eyes, so heavy were his eyes with color.

"What's the point of your campaign?" I turned the tables. "You have some great ideas, but if you don't intend to win or even try to win, then what's the point?"

"The point is to make a point."

"The point of flowers is pollination."

The bird's enthusiasm increased, and she began primping vehemently, clicking, murmuring, and softly croaking, her crumpling paper sound accelerating to angry librarians ripping up reference books. Her coat changed from fluffy to shining satin.

"What's your real name?" I threw at him. I knew his real name. I had researched it. I found his picture in the Apache College yearbook. He had graduated a year ago with a major in agriculture. The student directory showed his permanent address in Phoenix.

"My name is Henry David Tarantula."

"*Krapp*," said the raven.

He ignored the bird. "Pollination, huh? Then tell me why that spiny little hedgehog over there should sprout giant purple flowers in spring? Tiny ones would still attract the bugs." There was whistling from the bird and Henry David's chest. "Why should the air smell sweet in the morning? The sun turns the day to a white buzz." He was closing in on me. "Why do the mountains look blue in the distance? Distance to the feet means blisters." He was right in my face. "Why are your eyes so blue today?"

"Flowers are a gift," I answered.

Henry David's eyes turned light brown as if his soul cleared and inside was the desert, right when the rain let up, before the creatures started to move again.

The raven was serenading with grunts, groans, gurgles, moans, screeches, yells, strange dog-like growls then barking. Gasps, lisps, croaks and buzzing gulps.

"Do you know this bird?" I asked.

"She's a thief and a busybody. She steals my dishes right off my tree." He threw a cup at her. "Go away, Clementine." He missed but she yelled like a dog with her tail slammed in the kitchen door.

"How do you shut her up?"

"Give her money," he said. "She loves money."

I took a dollar bill out of my pocket and set it on the ground.

"*Errrrk*" like a needle coming to a screeching halt on a record.

"*Queek, queek, queek, kwulkulkul.*" No questions asked. She breezed down, grabbed the money and streaked off with a muffled "*quork, quork, quork.*"

Henry David grabbed me by my pale peach sundress and pulled me against him. He bent me backwards like an old-fashioned lover, pressing his hard lips into my neck, his fingers like pincers into my spine.

Clementine was back, flying high, then diving straight for us, something silver flashing. She thwacked Henry David on the head with a spoon.

It wasn't his gangly, hairless limbs and torso that set Clementine's velvety scalp on end. His dazzling nest of tangled hair might have made her lower feathers flutter. But I think it was his asthmatic wheezing, raven-like yelling and sultry harmonica that had arrested her normal sexual development and flung it in a deviant direction.

"She's in love with you," I said.

FROM THE JOURNAL OF HENRY DAVID TARANTULA

SEPTEMBER 1

I am a self-appointed inspector of clouds. This morning the sky is perfectly clear. I stand on my front porch, circling slowly, scanning for any tiny speck of moisture. I make three full turns. No promises. The high point of the zenith is a dark September blue, two shades deeper than royal July, the only hint that the sun is letting go.

Chapter 10

THE WINDOW

"Out of the dark I called to you; out of the enfolding
dark you came."
Struthers Burt, *"The Desert"*

For days it would cloud up in the afternoon and never rain. One evening
I thought it was finally going to happen, so I put a lawn chair in the front
yard and watched it coming. Blowing sand tore through my hair and
scoured my legs. Our garbage can sailed across the street and the wind
sucked grasshoppers straight up toward the jet stream. Still, it didn't come.
All August long I never got pelted, never had to run through water over
my ankles, counting seconds after lightning, clutching clothes so heavy
with rain they were sliding off. On the first of September, I made up my
mind. I would go to the Window.

The Window was a giant hole weathered in a rock formation near the
top of the San Miguel Mountains at the head of Cholla Canyon. It was a
vision quest site for the Apaches, who had a long tradition that recognized
the importance of dreams. If I could just look through the Window, maybe
I would learn what it was that I wanted so much.

My parents thought I was going to the annual Labor Day Weekend
Homecoming Party on Heck of a Hill. The Hill was a prominent butte on
the landscape just south of William that was marked with a big white "H"
near the summit. The H had been blazed by a brain-burned prospector in
the 1930s who probably meant something besides President Hoover,
though that's the story the Chamber of Commerce tells. The locals called
the landmark Heck of a Hill.

Keeping the H blindingly white was a solid tradition sponsored by the
Chamber and several Christian youth groups. Teenagers "whitewashed the
heck out of the hill" singing hymns, followed by a barbecue, bonfire and
camp-out at the nearby Boy and Girl Scout Camps.

With the opening of Apache College in 1970, the tradition was
modified a bit. The college students claimed the whitewashing event as
part of their Homecoming celebration, adding a little more H than the
Christians had ever conceived. They blazed a four-wheel drive trail up the
backside of the butte and parked a pick-up on top mounted with cinema-

sized speakers. They played the most metallic rock and rap, running the stereo off the truck battery. A serious amount of beer made its way to the barbecue and bonfire, and the students failed to respect the gender of the scout camping areas. Half-crocked incoming freshmen painted the H.

The event was whitewashed in the college's recruitment literature, and a full-page shot of the homecoming king and queen was always published in the yearbook. Cynthia had been a queen, of course. I thought the H was an eyesore. It was even more despicable now that the watermelon experimental farm was creeping around at its base.

"Time to swab down the old H again?" Daddy asked as I came into the kitchen early Saturday morning, my backpack over one shoulder. "The Chamber of Commerce is providing free watermelons. A little plug for my campaign."

"I hear it's going to be a really big party this year. You don't mind me keeping the International overnight?" I loaded a brown bag from the refrigerator into my pack. I had prepared my food the previous evening so I could get out in a hurry. A package of hot dogs, a bag of buns, squeeze bottle of mustard, marshmallows, two apples, and a pound of trail mix, plus a peanut butter and jelly sandwich for emergencies. It looked like I was going to a barbecue.

"Not at all. I can use your mother's car if I need to go somewhere. The weatherman said it might rain tonight. You should take an umbrella."

I rolled my eyes. I could see myself at a college campfire under a pink polka-dot umbrella. "I have my rain jacket." I filled up two quart-and-a-half canteens with water.

"That's a lot of water."

"Just in case."

Mom came into the kitchen in her intense red velour bathrobe. She didn't have to go to the office on Saturday. She must have had a better idea of the true nature of the Heck of a Hill party than Daddy because she pecked me good-bye on the cheek and quickly hissed in my ear, "Just don't get pregnant." I guess that was our little talk about the birds and bees.

"That's my girl," Daddy said as I kissed him good-bye. "Going where the action is. You'll make a great politician someday."

"A biologist, Daddy. I'm going to be a biologist."

Henry David figured I was going to Heck of a Hill also. I had seen him the previous Wednesday by the cave when I was watering.

"You're probably going to that stupid college party this weekend," he said.

"I wouldn't be caught dead at that party."

"You'll probably wear a pink party dress."

"It's a picnic for crap sake. Anyway, for your information, I'll be on the opposite side of the valley this weekend in the San Miguels, hiking up Cholla Canyon. I'm starting Saturday morning and camping out at Bridal Veil Falls. Then Sunday I'm going all the way to the Window. It's an Apache vision quest site."

He snorted. "You'll probably make out with some clean-cut greaseball of a college boy."

Nobody ever took me seriously. "I'll be wearing my hiking boots." I threw the watering can in the truck and boiled away in my flouncy lilac sunsuit.

I parked the International at the old Benson place at the base of Cholla Canyon where I had planted my Number Two experimental plot. I watered here on Tuesdays and Saturdays. The Benson plot was producing well. The first bloom had come a week ago, and now there was a flourish of orange and yellow. I measured stems and counted blooms. This would be the last entry for Benson, the experiment complete.

The plot was a full week ahead of the Caves site even though they were at the same elevation, about 1,000 feet above William. Benson sat on an alluvial fan that spilled out of the San Miguel Mountains north of town. The soil was alkaline, but less so than the limestone-permeated Santa Isabella Caves area to the east. Geologically speaking, Benson had more mature soil than the Caves. It was brick red and fine-grained like clay. Dominant plants were triangle-leaf bursage and cholla cactus.

Martha Benson had created flower gardens in a steadily growing perimeter around her house. I remember miniature roses growing on the swamp cooler trestle, honeysuckle climbing the windmill tower, foxglove waving at the mailbox out at the main road.

"All exotic species," I said aloud. I had watered my African daisies and was walking through Martha's stone-ringed, barren plots. I had been careful to plant in an area of untouched desert, away from any of Martha's flower beds, but I wondered if her ghostly influence might have something to do with my flourishing daisies.

It had been a decade since Martha had died in her little white house surrounded by a patchwork of colors. In the absence of relatives, the county auctioned off everything they thought was valuable to pay the taxes and promptly forgot about the place. The white paint had completely peeled from the clapboard house, which was now choked to the second story with Russian thistles. It had twisted on its foundation and partly caved in. The flowers were long gone. The windmill, ironically, had blown over. It still lay on its side, entwined with tumbleweeds instead of honeysuckle, probably unnoticeable if it weren't for the bright orange rust on the blades.

I put my empty watering can back in the truck and pulled on my backpack. I had been to the doorway of Cholla Canyon but had never walked into the mouth of it. I followed the dry channel of Cholla Creek. I was not a seasoned backpacker; I'd only read library books about it. I went to Girl Scout camp in fifth and sixth grades, which is why I even owned a sleeping bag. Daddy was not the hunting, fishing, camping type. He said he spent enough time in the great outdoors working construction. Mom landscaped with gravel, never kept houseplants, despised picnics, and kept a standing monthly appointment for the weed exterminator. Neither one would have approved this trip. There were insects out there, snakes, cougars, maybe strangers, or worse still, no other person.

"*Who-who? Who-who?*" Two mourning doves came in like satin and left like squeaky toys.

The seasons are a slow circle, always coming back to this same yellowed place, September. The desert dries up and shrinks to its simplest. The creek was a bed of rocks covered with the white skeletons of small leaves and a thin blanket of mineral precipitate like a gray papery moss. Cicadas sang in the palo verde trees. Out of sight of the Benson property, I caught a glimpse of the wildness that Martha faced as a young widow about 50 years ago. A forest of cholla. Nothing soft, forgiving or even approachable. Perhaps that explained her flight to flowers. I walked in the barren creek bed as it headed up into the San Miguels.

Passing through a Forest Service fence, I felt free, elated and hot. I took a quick break and squatted to pee, thinking I had everything so well planned and under control. It was then that I touched my left rear cheek to a cholla. A message from my mother? The dainty tweezers in my pocketknife proved useless. It took the knife blade and the *Peterson's Guide to Western Birds* in an incredibly contorted position to dislodge the prickly appendage. Mom had been telling me since high school, "Don't you dare ever come home with a tattoo."

The official Forest Service hiking trail started near the fence boundary, and I followed it as Cholla Canyon narrowed into a rocky hallway that the sun was not yet high enough to enter. I was suddenly in the shade. It was much cooler and the air was full of the muddy, leafy smell of water.

It was midday before I actually found a trace of that water. The trail cut through a grove of ancient cottonwoods. The trees were so huge I couldn't even wrap my arms around their circumferences. Cottonwoods, sacred trees to the Plains Indians because they pointed the way to water, were called "phreatophytes" in scientific circles—opportunists, free-loaders—because they sought water close to the surface and drew directly from the water table. In the center of the grove was a dark, stagnant pool. A few curled yellow leaves blew into the water and sailed north like tiny ships.

I got out my own water and sat down, gingerly, on a flat rock. There was a small, single, very white, fair weather cloud in the sky. I don't know where Daddy got the idea it was going to rain. I took a long drink and got out my notebook and my lunch. It didn't take long to record the cloud, eat an apple and a little trail mix. As I put the food bag and canteen away, I consulted the topo map. I was about halfway to the Window.

As I ascended from the depths of the canyon into the sunshine, the whirr of insects rose with me. Small birds or reptiles created a constant commotion in the brush. I was afraid to investigate because of the latter possibility. All afternoon I climbed the side wall of the twisting canyon on a steep trail lined with scree and shin daggers, the single cloud following over my left shoulder. The slopes were dotted with century plants and dry summer flowers with dark stems and burr-like petals. It was boiling hot, and I poured part of a canteen on my head and shirt. The hiking guides all said to synchronize your breathing with your walking, but I couldn't seem to control either. And always watch where you put your hands in the desert, because of cactus, scorpions and spiders. And where you put your ass, I added.

There was a point when I almost turned back. The canyon was closing in again, I could only walk a few steps before I had to stop and catch my breath, I had a stitch in my side, and the trail seemed to be hanging on the face of a cliff. Many rocks were encrusted with mica and they glittered like mirrors, making the height even more dizzying. Blue, soundless music bounded back and forth between the canyon walls. For a few panic-charged moments, I grasped two handfuls of Arizona cottontop grass, a three-foot-tall monocot, my right leg pumping up and down uncontrollably like a sewing machine. I wanted to go home, but I was afraid to look down, let alone turn around and walk down.

"Go to hell, wind," I yelled. Actually, there wasn't any wind, but it made me feel better.

I inched upward, clinging to the cliff in spite of the danger of sharp and poisonous handholds, trying to blot out the fact that I would have to come back down this way tomorrow. I passed burrows along the base of the rock wall, probably hollowed out by the flash of summer rains. They would make cozy nests for coyotes or rattlesnakes. I was relieved that they were empty.

The science project was a fake. A lark. A fantasy carried out in meticulous detail as I tried to make it real. I would probably even write up a lengthy report of my findings, but my biology teacher had never shown up at his office during the summer. We'd never had a conversation about a special project. He didn't even know my name.

A sharp whistle startled me. There, standing before me on top of a twenty-foot-tall saguaro, surely a good omen, was a bright red cardinal.

At last, Cholla Canyon dead-ended in a flat sandy area with a Forest Service sign announcing BRIDAL VEIL FALLS. In a wetter season, it would have been a spectacular, romantic, three-tiered cascade. Now the waterfall was bridal veil white with calcium carbonate and completely dry. Nor was there a drop of water in the stream that fed from it. This would be my campsite for the night. I was so amazed to have made it this far, I wasn't even disappointed by the absence of water.

"Follow the yellow brick road." I couldn't think of anything else to shout. "Follow the yellow brick road."

I took off my pack and shook my sweaty T-shirt away from my back. It was like a shot of air conditioning, enough to make me shiver. I had a broader view of the sky from up here. There were a few streaks of high gray stratus and the small white cloud that had been constant all day was now expanding upward.

Full of new energy, I laid out my sleeping pad and bag in the sand, remembering from the guidebook to keep a safe distance from the falls in case of a flash flood, then explored the vicinity for firewood. I soon had an armload of desert spoons and cactus skeletons. I made a circle of rocks, crumpled some paper from my notebook, arranged my sticks in a tepee around the paper, but didn't light it. Instead, suddenly and surprisingly non-acrophobic, I ascended the parched, stone course of the waterfall. Actually, it was only ten feet high. Near the top I found a natural recess, like a majestic throne in a vast imperial room. I climbed into it and surveyed the world at my feet.

"I'm a biologist," I yelled. I could see far across the valley all the way to Heck of a Hill. As the light faded, Venus appeared like a light blue beacon to the east. The cloud kept building. I began to think about insects, snakes and cougars. Javelina, too. What if I suddenly turned and looked into the face of a wolf? I pressed my back against the stone chair in the rock wall.

"My science project is a fake," I whispered.

South across the valley in the twilight I saw a small orange glow on the side of Heck of a Hill. The bonfire was lit. I could almost hear the gossip and giggling. To the east I pictured Henry David sitting naked in his cave dimly lit with the copper light of burning candles. It hadn't been an outright invitation for him to come, though I had certainly given him explicit information. But how silly to expect a rendezvous eight miles up a stickery canyon. The feeling of abandonment that hung on me like an elongated shadow was of my own making.

I slithered down from the waterfall, acrophobia back, and lit my own fire. It sprang up easily and yellow, bright and comforting as the air cooled and softened. I roasted two hot dogs in the flames, skewered on the old bone of a saguaro, and ate them with plenty of mustard. In the sunset, the white cloud was peachy, and as night fell, electricity fomented within it. It blinked like a firefly, buzzing toward the San Miguels.

When the flames of my campfire died to red coals, I speared two marshmallows on the saguaro stick and held them to the embers. All orange drained from the cloud, which was pulsating with electrical charge and coming closer, its underside outlined in bright white. Still no strikes descended on the valley.

Henry David glided into my camp not even a twig snapping. He slipped onto a rock, mostly a shape across the fire ring, his face a dark triangle. I could see some stars behind him, the Big Dipper and a slash of the Milky Way. I focused on the marshmallows, slowly turning them above the coals. Was Henry David real? Was he really here? My hair stood away from my head, sweating and restless to escape from my tight braid. Even the fine blond hairs on my arms came to attention and I felt prickles all the way down to my ankles.

Reaching across the coals with my stick, I offered Henry David my perfectly browned marshmallow candy. He plucked one marshmallow and consumed it with a low laugh. Still there, real. I took the other marshmallow. He darted around the fire and followed it into my mouth with a quick reptilian tongue. He had me by the braid and he pulled me over to my sleeping bag. My T-shirt disappeared like a young snake bursting out if its first skin. He flicked the rubber band from my hair and the waves cascaded around us both like a dark waterfall. He pushed me onto my back, tasted my earrings, and moved down my neck and chest taking little bites. He started chewing on the lace of my bra. My face was buried in the tangle of his hair, filling my nose, eyes and mouth with dust and pollen. I didn't know if he could feel my tender kisses on the top of his head.

There was a crash of thunder and Henry David bolted upward. His face was backlit by the flashing cloud, his hair flaming outward with static. I sat up, too, my waist-length hair even more frightening, the fine outer strands forming a huge halo of Saint Elmo's fire. A sudden wind blasted us with sand.

Henry David reached for the sleeping bag and draped it around our shoulders as we sat together facing the storm. Lightning cracked horizontally in huge spider webs across the sky. Henry David watched it like it was a sports show, chortling and rocking back and forth.

"Wow, look at that. Look at that."

But I never looked. I pressed my cheek against his smooth chest concentrating on every absentminded movement of his hand through my hair.

The sun, well beyond the horizon, threw back a blaze of magenta, firing the entire sky. Henry David nudged me away and I could see the lick of flames in his eyes.

"Tonight your eyes are midnight blue," he said. Then the sky lost its last color.

"Your father is a son of a bitch." That was his last comment as he melted into the dark.

I was damp and salty, exposed and freezing in the wind. I crawled into the sleeping bag and pulled it over my head. It wasn't waterproof, and I knew I was in trouble if the rain hit. Perhaps I should have brought the pink polka-dot umbrella after all. But the storm sailed above me and into the pine forest before dropping its water.

I dreamed of horses. Two or three large dark presences clattering up to me in the night. I was afraid they would step on me, but I was too tired to move, too sure it was a dream. They circled me, curious, and they communicated with a few quiet snorts and gentle whinnies. One bent over and nuzzled my face. They moved away and I heard them drinking. Then they were gone.

I awoke chilly in my sleeping bag. Water splashed down Bridal Veil Falls and chattered by me in the stream. The sky was opaque with low clouds, the air thick with humidity, the vivid smell of pine unleashed. What proof did I have? There were tiny red bites on my chest, but it could have been mosquitoes. My hair was a jumble of waves. Was it only the dampness? There were hoof prints in the sand all around me.

Still inside the bag, I fumbled through my pack for my sweatshirt and my hairbrush. Once warm, I loosened the tangles in my hair and tamed it back into a braid. Swallows dived against the backdrop of the white sky and a few threads of low fog drifted past my head like a woodwind lullaby. I ate an apple and a handful of marshmallows then stuffed my sleeping bag into the bottom of my pack. I checked the ashes from my campfire, and they were completely cold. Lying on my belly, I dipped my face into the newly reborn stream and drank.

I got back on the trail and it switch backed quickly above Bridal Veil Falls and into the trees. Soon I was also in the clouds. It was like a vagueness closing in around me, and I could only see clearly a few feet ahead. I followed the trail on faith. Then, gaining a little elevation, I was back in the sunshine, hot and buzzing, the clouds below me now, filling the valley like a fluffy blanket. It was so tempting to believe I could leave the trail, step off onto the clouds and stay afloat, instead of plummeting into the bottom of Cholla Canyon. With all that moisture, there was sure to be rain down in William tonight.

The Window came unexpectedly. I almost stumbled into it. I steadied myself with both hands on its lower ledge. I closed my eyes and tried to regulate my breathing, my heart pounding from the hike and the elevation. The ledge was smooth, rubbed by wind, rain and human hands. I leaned into it on my elbows, resting. I didn't know how to calm the constant prattle inside my brain. Get your head out of the clouds, forget your dreams, don't be silly. I wasn't ready. I wasn't worthy. Then I heard music.

There must be a small fissure somewhere in the rock formation, and a rise in the wind played through it like a blues harmonica. I opened my eyes and looked through the Window. All I could see was clear blue sky.

FROM THE JOURNAL OF HENRY DAVID TARANTULA

JUMPING CHOLLA

Coming down the Cholla Canyon Trail at night with a flashlight was not a problem, the white rocks magnifying the light, until I reached the forest of cacti at the bottom. Every field guide will tell you cholla don't really jump, but one leapt onto my elbow as I passed a far distance away from it. I couldn't shake it off, my thin elbow skin sagging under its weight. I ran to get away, but it followed like a flying pincushion, like a woman after me. The faster I ran the more they came at me. Thank goodness for my goggles. I had one branch on the toe of each shoe and one on top of the left one, trying to get inside. The demon cholla were throwing their arms at me like some wicked way of waving. Yelling seemed to make me more of an attractant, and I must have stirred up the pollen because I began sneezing, too. By the time I reached the flower truck, my shirt and shorts were festooned with brambled appendages. I ditched my clothes on the road and drove back to the cave naked.

Chapter 11

THE FLOWER DELIVERY

"If you have any doubt about it, know that the desert begins with the creosote."
Mary Austin, *The Land of Little Rain*

The rain finally came to William on Sunday, a steady pummeling all night long with low rumbles of thunder in the distance. On Monday morning, Labor Day, I took my last measurements at the plot near the Caves, recording my very first rain, 0.6 inches. It was a day later and an hour earlier than my usual schedule, but what did it matter? I jotted observations in my notebook.

Cloud Report: Cottony clouds still stuck to the eastern horizon. The sun rose, socked in. I waited for color, but there was no red or pink or orange, not even light yellow. The sunrise was completely white.

The African daisy seeds had germinated quickly. Twelve days. It said ten to thirty on the seed packet. Now, at thirty-four days, I was expecting them to be approaching full height, about ten inches. They were still hovering at three or four, though a few of them had flowered. I had to lie in the mud to measure them. I collected my rain gauge and, locating a hammer and nail in the toolbox in the back of the International, I pounded a note to Henry David into the trunk of the pecan tree.

I noticed that Henry David's porch was littered with beer cans. Clementine was creating a racket with them, rolling, hammering, clucking and sputtering, once again driving Henry David outside. This time he was more modestly clad in a T-shirt, forearm over his eyes. He was alert enough to stay away from the saguaro, but in staggering the other direction, he went right into the arms of the catclaw, whose intricate fingernails stitched him in place as securely as Gulliver by Lilliputians.

"*Trill, trill, warble, spor-rick-ruck, unk, unk, gong.*" Clementine's head feathers stood on end.

"You big black bird, you pecker at my window, you player on the wind, go to hell, wind. Leave me alone." This was loud enough to produce an echo. Then Henry David soaked the catclaw with the business for which he had ventured out in the first place.

"Dear Henry David," my note said. "You son of a bitch. Why did you leave me up there on the mountain? You want to be Thoreau. Why don't you just be yourself? You're more afraid than I am. Go to hell. Virginia. P.S. My experiment is over."

That afternoon, after conducting T-tests on my neat columns of growth data, I rejected the null hypothesis and accepted the alternative: Alkalinity is negatively correlated with the growth of African daisies, a hardy annual. I typed my final report.

Conclusions: This is the most absurd science project ever. A more meaningful experiment would have been to simply pluck the petals off a random African daisy: He loves me, he loves me not, he loves me, he loves me not . . .

That evening the delivery was made. The lavender Flower Shoppe truck clambered into our driveway, and Henry David wearing motorcycle goggles knocked on the front door. Mom was in the kitchen getting dinner ready, and Daddy and I were in the living room watching the news on TV. Daddy answered the door.

"These are for Virginia," Henry David said, handing over a bundle of greenery wrapped in newspaper and tied with string.

"Who the H are you?"

But Henry David didn't answer. He jumped back in the truck and peeled away.

The Flower Shoppe went out of business about six months ago. I had called the number in the phone directory and gotten the disconnected message. I drove by their listed address. The lavender storefront was now just a lavender home, but there was a greenhouse in the back. I walked around and tapped on the glass door.

A white-haired gentleman invited me in, and I asked about *Dimorphotheca aurantiaca*, African daisy, a hardy annual. He thumbed through a thick horticultural manual with brown-stained hands, and he told me the history of his flower business. It was a mom-and-pop operation and he (Pop) just got too old to keep up with the competition, though he still liked to hum and cluck among his orchids and roses.

"But I've recently seen your flower truck on the road," I said.

"Sold it to a young fella who used to work for me as a delivery man. Mom didn't like him at all. His hair was long and frizzy, and he wore motorcycle goggles when delivering flowers. Said it was his allergies. Mom didn't buy it."

His false teeth clicked a bit.

"Those two went at it a couple of times. Finally, she fired him when she found out he told a bereaved customer to go to hell. She nearly canned me when I sold him the old truck."

I had a clue to his apparent affinity for Henry David. His fine white hair lifted and flitted in the warm, damp air of the greenhouse.

"*Dimorphotheca*," he read from the book, "means two shapes of seed. The plant has two non-identical seed forms. Thrives in well-drained soil, full sun. Does not prosper in too hot of weather."

"I wonder if that's why my flowers aren't doing too well. I planted them at the beginning of August. But the packet said planting season was May through September."

"Sometimes you can't force flowers. It's just too late. Next time try May. Or even March around here. There's just something about spring for birth and rebirth." He went back to reading the botany book. "Natives of South Africa. Many varieties from the original wild types. Blooms in pale and dark yellows, salmons and apricots or white. It has naturalized throughout the southwestern U.S."

"Naturalized," I said. "So, it's no longer considered an exotic?"

"So he's still driving the old truck?"

Who the H was that?" Daddy asked as he handed me the bundle. I had peered out the curtains in the living room when he answered the front door. "He looked like a hippie hood."

"That was Henry David Tarantula."

"Son of a bee. How do you know him?"

"I met him through the college. He used to go to there and I heard him give a political speech."

"Why didn't you say something before? What's his platform? How does he expect to win anything looking like that?"

"I don't think he expects to win. You're going to win. He's no match for you."

Daddy went back to watching the TV, frowning.

I took Henry David's package into my bedroom and pulled off the string. When I had hiked out of Cholla Canyon and seen his cactus-studded clothes on the side of the road, I first thought Henry David might have been hit by lightning and vaporized. The newspapers held a bouquet of creosote branches. The tiny leaves were green and waxy, and the pinched yellow buds had opened with the storm. They filled my room with the smell of rain.

There was a note inside the package that was scrawled almost illegibly. It took me a few minutes to realize that the script ran from right to left across the page and was completely backwards, like mirrored writing. "Soon your father and his posse will come to ambush my cave. You won't come up here to live with me. You'd rather stay in the city with that beer can old man and you don't love me."

Mom called that dinner was ready. It was obvious that Daddy had already spoken with her as both of them emitted a suspicious silence during the entire meal. Monday was always spaghetti night, and Mom didn't have an ounce of Italian blood in her. Ground beef, tomato sauce and noodles, period. At least she had recently cultivated the habit of picking up dinner rolls from the Italian bakery on her way home from work.

"You never told us about the Homecoming party," Mom finally said as she poured coffee after the meal for Daddy and herself. She used a honeyed tone. "Cynthia said her friend Jean said she never saw you at the party all night."

"Not much to tell."

"I forbid you to see Henry David Tarantula," Daddy said. No extra sugar in his cup tonight and no sweetness in his voice.

"He's going to be pretty hard to avoid if I participate at all in your campaign. He's a candidate."

"You know what I mean."

"We're talking about family loyalty here," Mom said.

"Henry David Tarantula is opposed to watermelon farming. I support him on that. My science project confirms the unsuitability of soils in that area."

"Watermelons mean progress for this town." Daddy snapped into his campaign rhetoric. "I stand on a solid platform of watermelons."

"We're talking about family loyalty here," Mom said again. Her voice was laced with black coffee, and that was the end of the conversation.

Chapter 12

CHIHUAHUA
"It is life near the bone where it is sweetest."
Henry David Thoreau, *Walden*

Across the foothills of Chihuahua, Trap cut a swath of crime and destruction. He robbed dog bowls of beans and tortillas, ransacked garbage and gobbled chickens. His injured lower leg soon withered, but his right thigh that carried the weight of the trap was like steel. His chest and forelegs, which bore the brunt of his long runs, became massive. By October, he was taking on full-grown cows.

Trap always worked at night and always went for the throat. His victims had no chance to call out, and the ranchers of the foothills were more terrorized by this silence than by the bloody carcasses he left behind. People grew afraid of the dark and many, in nightmares, imagined they could hear a chain rattling.

Señor Raven worked only by day. At night he slept near the top of a dead tree at the edge of the foothills, facing east, head nearly submerged in his feathers. At first light he set out after Trap, and by following the wolf's tracks or fresh excrement, he regularly had a bountiful breakfast. In fact, the raven grew quite portly. His ominous appearance in the aftermath of the kills, solemn, preened and sleek as a mortician, gained him infamy in his own right. The district newspaper, in a not-so-subtle dig at the head of the Bureau of Taxation, dubbed him Eduardo.

By the end of October, the Sierra Madres were touched with snow. Cold air settled in the canyon bottoms and icy winds ripped across the ridges. Trap's fur grew luscious and velvety, plenty of protection against any extreme temperature, if it hadn't been for the trap. His right leg ached in the cold and was as stiff as the frozen metal in which it was caught. Even the foothills, though warmer, seemed barren and dismal until one night at a stone wall that formed a fortress around a large ranch house, he caught the scent of a female in heat.

Trap paced the entire circumference of the wall, whining and planting his scent on hers. He thrust his nose through the wrought iron gates searching for her odor on the air, lusting for her thick fur and her hot breath. Only at dawn did he retreat to the mountains. There, on a high rock, he threw his head back to the early morning and wailed and wailed, his tongue moving up and down like a trombone slide.

"*Ah-ooooh-ah-y-wuh-wuh-wuh-wuh-wuh.*"

The whole mountainside seemed to hush as the sound rushed down to the foothills. The rancher got on the telephone and began to organize a wolf hunt. His wife cried and prayed, and the female dog paced and whined at the door.

To the dismay of Señor Eduardo, the lovesick wolf forsook hunting for the next three nights in favor of whimpering at the wall and urinating on the gates of his prospective mate. And each dawn he howled his troubles to the sky, giving away his general location to the ranchers who were plotting his death. On the fourth night, the wolf would wait no longer and neither would the ranchers. Trap began digging at the back gate as a line of pickup trucks drove up to the hacienda and parked in front.

It was almost daybreak when Trap squeezed his flattened body under the iron bars. As he came up nose first on the other side, anxiously straining for a whiff of the female, he raised his back leg too soon and snagged the trap. The boisterous noises of men going on a wolf hunt—doors slamming, shouting, a dog barking (his future mate?), the front gate clanging, heavy objects banging into the pickups—covered the frantic rattling of the back gate as the wolf tried to free himself. The ranchers piled into two of the trucks and headed into the mountains, leaving the wolf alone at the hacienda. Alone except for the bitch in heat who had been shut inside. The rancher's wife, barely enduring two mornings of Trap's fearful howling, had taken the children and driven to the city to her mother's.

After several hours of painful pulling and one furious wrenching, the wolf was suddenly released and he rolled hard into the yard.

"*Oof.*"

He stood up feeling light and off balance and crashed once more. The heavy trap no longer figured into his body English. It, along with his emaciated lower leg, hung on a wrought iron bar of the gate. Trap reeled about the bushes and garden in the ecstasy of freedom, gaining coordination on three legs, filling his nostrils with the female aroma. From inside the house came a high-pitched whine, and Trap flung his body through a picture window.

There, in the middle of the huge living room of the ranch house, running around on top of a grand piano, was a white, spotted Chihuahua.

Though she reeked of sexual rhapsody, she had the legs of a chicken, the eyes of a bug, the coat of a bald javelina, and her ears flapped like bird wings. She ran in small circles like a frightened mouse and yapped in a key that gave Trap a headache.

Trap took all he wanted from her—the beans and tortillas in her bowl. Then he did something no wolf had done for thirty-five years. He got on the road and headed north. Eduardo followed.

FROM THE JOURNAL OF HENRY DAVID TARANTULA

POLITICS

I am not interested in politics. Rather philosophy. The pure strain of ideas. Politics is salesmanship, bleating at sheep, winking at the media, kissing. Selling what people want to hear, not what people should think. It's an art of the body, not the mind. The great political philosophers—Plato, Heroditus, Marx—would never have grinned at a camera or sucked up to a potential contributor. Philosophy lives in the clouds, in the caves. This morning the sky is plastered with small cumulus. Each has a tail of rain which never even dreams of reaching the ground.

Chapter 13

PRESS CONFERENCE

"I'm sure I've never read any memorable news in a newspaper."
Henry David Thoreau, *Walden*

At the beginning of November, exactly one week before the general election, the League of Women Voters held its traditional candidate's forum at the Town Hall. It was an off year as far as Presidential, Gubernatorial and Senate elections, and Congressional candidates never stumped in William. The local political scene was really in the doldrums, with the Clerk, Assessor, Clerk of Court, Treasurer and Sheriff all running unopposed. The mayoral race was the only contest with any pizzazz, and this was mostly because very few people had ever even seen the challenger.

As Daddy often said in his campaign speeches, "Who the H is Henry David Tarantula?"

Town Hall was bedecked with red, white and blue balloons and large tissue paper flowers manufactured by elderly ladies in afternoon work sessions. At one end of the long room was a raised stage upon which stood a table and podium festooned with twisted crepe paper streamers. Behind the table was a line of metal folding chairs for the candidates and their families.

Since the League's forum was the first glimpse the media had of Henry David, they arrived in mass. Two local television crews strung high intensity lights from the rafters and set up a bank of microphones at the podium. They staked out a wide lane for their cameras directly behind the front row of reporters. The radio stations and newspaper people, all wearing blazers, had their tape recorders on the speakers' table and were jotting down background color in their steno pads. There were orange extension cords running all over the room.

We arrived early. We had to allow extra time for Cynthia in the bathroom. She was five months pregnant, already looked like she had swallowed a watermelon, and still complained of morning sickness. She could have been a poster girl for WM, Inc. in her bright red maternity blouse. I had just spent fifteen minutes sitting on the sink at the Town Hall ladies' room while she retched and groaned inside a stall. Cynthia loved throwing up. She had become infatuated with the power and drama of it at about age ten and had been using it to keep her weight down ever since. I'm surprised Mom hadn't figured that out yet. Even more inexplicable: I'd been holding Cynthia's hand since I was six, though it gave me the dry heaves.

"Breathe, Cyn, breathe," I chanted from outside the stall door.

"*Goddamncrapsuckingsonofabitch,*" she yelled back at me.

At least she helped me fix my hair. I wanted it less severe than my usual braid, so she parted it in the middle, twisted the sides softly away from my face and held them back with dark combs studded with tiny rhinestones. She left the rest to spill in dark curves over my shoulders.

"You should wear your hair like this more often, Gin. You'd get a boyfriend in no time." She annoyingly fidgeted with my dress, too, and insisted that I put on a bit of her vermillion lipstick.

"This looks better on you with your dark hair. I'm just too blonde." Cynthia had been enhancing her light brown hair with bleach since sixth grade, and Mom and Daddy still seemed to be none the wiser.

Daddy wore his medium blue sports jacket that really brought out his eyes, and Mom sat at his right hand in her winter white suit, smiling. Cynthia sat down on Mom's right along with her hovering husband Everett who had obviously just gotten a haircut. Everett had removed his sports jacket and folded it up to cushion suffering Cynthia's plump rear end. Everett, on the other hand, was turning into a beanpole, but I liked his bolo tie. I sat on Daddy's left, next to the one chair that was available for the opposition party. I hadn't seen Henry David since early September, and I had a drop of desert primrose perfume behind each ear. I had steadfastly refused to conform to the red, white and blue motif, wearing a Kelly green dress with tiny checks and a narrow band of crocheted lace at the throat, thinking I was making an environmental statement. It suddenly came to me in a horrified wave that Kelly green was the color of watermelon skin.

"We didn't leave your friend much space for family," Daddy whispered to me. "Do tarantulas have siblings? Maybe his mother is a black widow." That gave him a chuckle.

Right at noon Henry David arrived in a red Hawaiian shirt splashed with blue and white tropical flowers and big pink birds. The cameras rolled.

An audible gasp and whisper came from Cynthia. "That shirt is positively disgusting."

"Completely inappropriate," Mom agreed.

Henry David brought with him an old-fashioned window-insert air conditioner, which he put on the table next to the speaker's podium. He plugged it into the power strip that was feeding the microphones. Without saying a word, he walked back out into the hallway, returning momentarily with a sledgehammer.

Daddy didn't wait for the presiding Woman Voter to introduce the session or present the first question. He leapt to the microphone and began in polished political tone.

"My friends, if I'm re-elected mayor I promise you that I will rid this area of all the free-loading cave dwellers." He looked directly at Henry David. "Who knows what filth they live in. You can be sure they're not doing an honest day's work. We'll flush them out and move them back into the city where they belong."

Hearty applause was provided by two rows of businessmen Daddy had planted in the audience. Cynthia whispered to Mom, "That guy's shirt makes me want to puke."

Henry David switched on the air conditioner. He had tied survey flagging to the vents in the front and they flapped in the humming breeze. The sound system went berserk and set up a feedback chain that had all attendees pressing their hands over their ears. The media members were on their feet and yelling. Cynthia screamed.

"Hey, you're messing up our equipment."

"We can't tape over that racket."

"Turn that thing off."

"This is the best way to turn off an air conditioner." Henry David swung the sledgehammer over his head and let it down on the machine with a mighty whack. The knobs and front flew off, the sound system howled, and the reporters jumped back.

"The only good air conditioner is a dead air conditioner. They're polluting the environment. As your mayor, I would clean them out of this town." The machine was now stuttering and squeaking.

Daddy pulled the plug on it, which probably won him a few of the "uncertain" votes, and usurped the microphones again.

"Would you mind, sir, if I take this machine back home with me to my shop since it is now useless as an air conditioner?"

He faced the cameras and continued in his most instructional voice.

"This air conditioner contains bits of copper, aluminum, brass and steel. Probably only about twenty-five cents worth, but all metals can be recycled, and it is a violation of the highest environmental principles to destroy a piece of equipment like this and leave it unrecycled."

"You're no environmentalist. You're a fraud." The microphone didn't pick this up, but I knew Mom would hate Henry David forever.

"But now for a bit of good news," Daddy said with a big smile. He leaned forward as if he were telling a secret. "I have it directly from WM, Inc., our fruitful friends who are growing those luscious watermelons south of town at the experimental farm." He leaned back as if delivering a punchline. "The second harvest begins tomorrow."

"This is making me hungry," Cynthia loudly whispered, to Everett this time. He gave her a sweet smile and gently patted her tummy. Now *I* felt like puking.

As if the Fourth of July crop of U.S. Fancy grade Desert Hallelujah watermelons wasn't water-consumptive enough, WM, Inc. had squeezed in a second planting of a hybrid icebox melon—shorter growing season, cooler temperature tolerant—called Sugar Daddy.

Henry David interrupted before Daddy could promote the Sugar Daddies. "Watermelons, humbug. Those fatso fruits are sucking up the water of future generations and they're displacing the natural desert creatures—the rattlesnakes, the scorpions, the tarantulas..."

"Now I ask you, my friends," Daddy said, nudging his way back into the microphone, "which would you rather have on your dinner table? A watermelon or, ha ha, a scorpion?"

Whistles, laughter and applause erupted from the businessmen and there was a snicker among the press as they frantically noted, TARANTULA WANTS SCORPIONS FOR DINNER.

"I'd rather have a glass of water on the table and a scorpion in the desert where it belongs." The comeback scarcely noticed.

"Mr. Tarantula, if you're elected, do you plan to raise the water rates?" To the surprise of all, a young newspaper reporter had stood up and asked a serious, intelligent question.

"First of all, I don't plan to get elected." That set the press a-buzz again.

TARANTULA PREDICTS OWN DEFEAT. The reporters were envisioning front page headlines already.

"You ridiculous reporters and pompous politicians can't understand that, can you? Most candidates, no matter how minuscule their chances for election, waddle right up to the platform and proclaim first off that they're going to win. What a stupid thing to say. I guess they get a lot of stupid people to vote for them that way. Winning is not important. Ideas are important. An election is one of the only free forums left in this country. Nobody goes to the park anymore."

Henry David's Jimmy Stewart drawl was becoming more pronounced, and I could see that he was luring at least the young reporter when Daddy interrupted.

"As I was saying." Daddy cleared his throat and resumed his hearty Chamber of Commerce tone. "Tomorrow begins another successful harvest. What has started as a small experimental operation is expected to double, quadruple and even sextuple in a few years. Now *that's* progress."

He had accidentally let the syllable "sex" slip out, and he nervously glanced back at Mom hoping she hadn't caught it. She was still smiling, but I knew she'd nail him later.

"Yes, I'd raise the water rates," Henry David was trying to get back to his point, "On industry, not for the local people. I'd sextuple them."

Desperately steering away from sex, George burst in. "WM, Inc. is donating a truckload of melons to show the local folks their appreciation for your support of their new industry. So come on over to the Paradise Mall this weekend for free watermelon. I'll be there all-day Sunday slicing."

The prepared audience was responding with enthusiastic applause. Mom had coached him in the car about the importance of getting in the ideas of God and prayer in school. I didn't think he was going to make it, but he thrust himself into the microphone one more time.

"Please keep watermelons in your prayers."

Henry David slung the sledgehammer over his shoulder, leaned toward me, lingering a moment on the perfume, and whispered, "Harvest tomorrow. I guess I'll be needing this hammer tonight." Then he slipped out the door.

Helen Kingsley, president of the League of Women Voters, finally found an opening at the podium. She had trim gray hair and wore a neat navy pantsuit. She had to pull the microphone way down to her petite height. Her diction was perfect.

"My dear ladies and gentlemen. This has been quite a remarkable evening. Our two mayoral candidates have clearly defined the issues that challenge us in the upcoming election. Should we clean out the caves—or the air conditioners? Should we support—or squash—watermelons?

They have also posed a deep philosophical question for us all to ponder over the next week: What is the true spirit of environmentalism?"

She was the kind of woman that made me want to stand up straight and take my hands out of my pockets. But the press had no manners. They stampeded past her and swamped Daddy. Cameras began flashing in our faces.

FROM THE JOURNAL OF HENRY DAVID TARANTULA

CATERPILLAR

The plan was completely flaky, hatched during the tail end of a boondocker on a Saturday night. Guys were slugging down quart bottles of Bud and talking tough against the line of yellow Caterpillar bulldozers parked alongside us in the Sanctum Sanctorum, our favorite party location out in the desert east of William. In the morning, cactus and creosote would be ripped up to make way for the new Paradise Mall. The booze made us all much bigger than reality, especially in the brains department, our rippling muscles real matches for the heavy equipment operators who would show up tomorrow. Our talk was mostly foam. As the clock ticked past midnight and we were all supposed to be back to the dorms by one o'clock, guys became more interested in putting their marks up the skirts of the sleepy coeds. Besides, the only tool we could come up with among us was a black magic marker. Couple after couple slunk away in spite of my exhortations about saving the desert and my accusations that they would become the biggest shoppers at Paradise. I stayed till three, then went to work on the bulldozers alone. My first crude political statement, "Cock suck nibble chew." The judge said I was lucky the cops hadn't shaved my head and the construction workers hadn't given me a tattoo. The college suspended me for a semester. My mother whined, "It's just a college prank." My father told me not to come home. What no one realized: I was the Caterpillar. And I had burst out of my cocoon.

Chapter 14

THE WATERMELON PLOT

"Disobedience is the true foundation of liberty. The obedient must be slaves."
Henry David Thoreau, *Journal, 1847*

The Sugar Daddy watermelon plants had grown like Jack's beanstalk across the 10-acre experimental farm. Their elephantine leaves had covered the fields within a few weeks of their planting, and the eight-foot-high chain link wall that surrounded the property could not completely contain them. Their tentacles had climbed the southern fence and spread up the side of Heck of a Hill. That acre or so of out-of-bounds growth was the patch WM, Inc. had bombastically offered to donate to the local residents.

WM had promised a water-saving drip irrigation system—eventually. But during the experimental stage, they were using old-fashioned flooding to water the crop. They pumped water from the underground aquifer, discretely purchasing the water rights on 100 acres to feed the 10. Every four days, the pumps went on at nine o'clock in the evening, after the air had cooled, and water poured down concrete ditches till midnight, spilling out into the field covering it with a full inch of water. By dawn the plants had soaked up the moisture and were making melons. Each day the leaves transpired approximately .3 inches of water from their broad leaves. The moisture readily evaporated during the warm autumn, but in the cool twilights, it condensed into a waist-high mist.

I waited until after six o'clock in the evening when the foreman had gone home, the honeybees had retreated to their hives, and the mist was rising. I wore the white poetry dress to blend with it and left my special-agent trench coat in the truck. That was a mistake. While daytime temperatures were still in the eighties, at night they plunged way below the comfort level of a dress that was more like a dresser scarf. I had borrowed the bright blue International to "go to the library" and parked it beyond the WM headquarters building, out in the desert under a palo verde tree. There was a beaten trail just outside the south fence line and I followed that. My light blue Keds left no tracks. When I got to the place where the vines had bolted over the fence, I headed up Heck of a Hill hauling a large black plastic bag of supplies.

Nothing I was doing was illegal. This was not private property but public land. It was the watermelons that were trespassing. In a sense, what I was doing was highly moral. It might even be considered environmental art. Once the light reached its most equivocal state, I began my work just below the H. I had seven cans of dazzling white spray paint, one for each letter. I sprayed quickly and then slipped down into the mist among the trespassing melons. Here the more detailed phase began, and I used a thick Japanese brush and tubes of fluorescent acrylics. After two hours of crawling around in the wet leaves, it no longer seemed like a lark. I was freezing cold. When I finally finished, it was fully dark.

As I was gathering my equipment to leave, I heard a car door. I dove back into the watermelon patch. Now I wished I were wearing a black turtleneck, maybe a black wool turtleneck, and dark jeans. Someone was walking down the fence line. I peered out from behind the leaves and recognized the Hawaiian shirt, the white flowers glowing in the dark.

I couldn't make out Henry David's face. He must have darkened it with charcoal and he had a dark cap pulled down over his hair. Instead of heading up Heck of a Hill in my direction, he climbed over the south fence onto private property. I heard his sledgehammer clang against the chain link. Squashing melons on private property was definitely more serious. He could end up in jail. Once Henry David was in the watermelon patch, the shirt was good camouflage. He dropped into the irrigation ditch and I lost sight of him.

I wanted no witnesses either. I had brought an extra black plastic garbage bag with me. I wrapped that around my shoulders and waited. Minutes passed. Then maybe an hour. I was still damp but now warm under the plastic and the plants. The fog seemed to be thickening out in the main field, but up on the hillside where I was hunkered, it was clearing. The Latin species name for watermelon is *Citrullus lanatus* of the family Cucurbitaceae. The flowers are unisexual. Like the African daisy, the watermelon had its origins in southern Africa. The first recorded watermelon harvest was in Egypt nearly 5,000 years ago. The ideal soil for watermelon growth has a pH value of 6.0 to 6.8, quite acidic. How was this experimental farm different from my own science project? An invasive idea visited on the sensitive landscape for my own selfish purposes. Did the desert need daisies, naturalized or not? What is the point of beauty? The air was still.

I was not alone and I'm not talking about Henry David. The leaves were moving. They reached toward me touching the bare skin of my neck and legs with their rough, itchy undersides. Twice a tentacle crawled up behind my ear. A net of vines tightened around me. The watermelon patch was a living, breathing presence. I could hear it whispering. As the hour wore on, it seemed more restless, prowling, murmuring, perhaps impatient for irrigation water. Would the melons become belligerent? Any minute I expected them to start heaving and thumping on themselves. A dull punk sound indicates full ripeness. What was Henry David waiting for anyway, the moon?

Yes. At last, the full moon poured out from the horizon. The H on Heck of a Hill lit up and moonbeams began flowing downward toward the melon patch. Henry David stood up in the ditch. I could see him quite clearly in the moonlight. He was writhing and twisting, not at all discreet.

"Get off of me you creepy crawlers," he yelled. Once free, he put on his motorcycle goggles and pointed up at the H. "It's gonna mean Hell tonight."

Henry David raised the sledgehammer over his head, he was about to mash melons, when something caught his attention on the hillside. With one hand, he lifted his goggles to see better. The moonlight was picking up some new letters below the H. WM SUCKS. Relentlessly, the light moved downward, now revealing luminous leering heads hanging haphazardly on the hillside. They had pink gaping mouths, flailing tongues, and eyebrows like lightning. I'd done a magnificent job creating watermelon jack o'lanterns. I stood up, shocked by my own handiwork.

It was nine o'clock on an irrigation night and the water pump came on with the throaty roar of a large diesel engine. I grabbed my plastic garbage bag filled with empty paint cans, came down the hill fast, and started running down the fence line. I don't know if it was the fluorescent watermelons, my white floating dress, or the clanging cans that scared Henry David, but he started screaming.

"Ghosts. Ghosts."

The wall of irrigation water hit him in the knees and toppled him like a toy duck. I could hear him and his sledgehammer banging down the concrete ditch. A thought hit me, too, like a ton of water. It was about time for me to get out of town, and I knew where I was going. I raced for the bright blue International.

FROM THE JOURNAL OF HENRY DAVID TARANTULA

I planned to stay in this cave for one year, and I have stayed longer. But now my experiment is over. The ragweed and mulberry spore are overpowering me and the dampness of winter is settling into my lungs. I am filling up again with water. Yet, I am free. In my dreams I'm a white wolf running, running all night. To go faster I run on my back legs. When my legs tire, I run on my hands.

Chapter 15

THE ELECTION
"Even voting for the right is doing nothing for it. It is only expressing to men feebly your desire that it should prevail."
Henry David Thoreau, *"Civil Disobedience"*

It must have been the full moon. All the tricksters were out. I crept onto my own street in neutral, headlights off, still shivering from the watermelon patch, pausing one house down from ours to make sure the coast was clear. If the living room and kitchen were dark, my parents were in bed and I would pull into the driveway. The lights were out, but something else was amiss. Right across the street from our house was a large, dark sedan loaded with people. I don't think they even noticed my quiet entry. I waited at the neighbor's, curious, and rolled my window down.

Four doors opened simultaneously and the inside of the car lit up. I recognized two of them immediately. Town Councilmen Michael A. Sherwood and John T. McMahon. Mike and Mack, probably drinking out of a paper bag. The guys my dad hung around with in politics certainly weren't the same caliber as Captain Corti and Lieutenant Lane of the fire department.

Two people I didn't recognize rolled out of the back seat. One was a woman with big, red hair and very high heels. She took off her coat and threw it back into the car. Her dress was as light and summery as my own, and it dipped drastically in front with her heavy endowment spilling out into the moonlight. A young man with a video camera was the fourth passenger. He didn't say a word, just slipped across the street and crouched behind the peach tree in front of our house.

"Wait, Millie, let's fill your glass," Mack said. He produced a champagne flute and, sure enough, filled it from a paper bag.

As Millie made her wobbly way across the street and up the sidewalk to our front door, the two councilmen were doubled over and snorting at the car.

"We'll really get the goods on Old Goody Two-Shoes George tonight."

"He'll be dashing to save his *own* can now."

Daddy must have thought it was the fire department. He opened the front door in his undershirt, baggy shorts and skinny legs. He still wore his socks to bed.

I couldn't hear their conversation, though Millie was gesturing with the champagne glass. Soon she had her breasts to his eyeballs trying to shove her way into our house.

"Dot...Dot...Dot..." That part I could hear.

Daddy grabbed Millie by the neck and pushed her back out toward the street. Mom came from behind Daddy and charged out into the yard. It would have made some great footage: My mom, an adrenalin-drenched hissing blonde with Daddy's ancient 20-gauge single shot shotgun. A much better video than the one that had obviously been planned of my dad with the redhead. But it looked like the cameraman was splayed flat in the tree well. No shot was fired. Daddy wrestled the gun away from Mom, and four people never got into a car so fast. I slid down under the International steering wheel.

The next morning Mom had already left for work when I came bleary-eyed into the kitchen. In fact, she had already been to the grocery store and back with a stack of newspapers. Daddy was elated about the press conference coverage, and he had coffee and the front page all ready for me.

He was so photogenic. There he was on the banner of the morning *Star*, arms up in victory, his eyes looking so blue even in the black and white photo. Underneath Daddy's arm, you could see my face in the background. I had his dark hair and dark eyebrows. I was the only family member in the picture. At the bottom of the page was a small, blurry photo of Henry David in his Hawaiian shirt. The paper called him Spiderman, never even bothering to research his real name.

"Your Mom thinks someone is out to get me." That was all he said about last night's redhead. "But nothing's going to go wrong now. It's less than a week until the election. This one is sewn up."

I felt like I had a hangover though I had never in my life drunk more than the foam off Daddy's beer. I was about to pop his campaign balloon.

The melons hit the headlines in the evening *Citizen*: WATERMELON CROP LOOKS BAD. A ghoulish Sugar Daddy had captured the front-page photo. And in the next morning's *Star*: HECK OF A WATERMELON CROP HARVESTED YESTERDAY. Neither paper mentioned the specific verbiage of the hillside message. I wondered if they were subject to FCC regulations.

The *Star* said, "Some graffiti painted on the hillside by the vandal or vandals was cleaned up by a few volunteer firemen." It was not vandalism, it was revolution! I kept telling myself. The *Citizen* never mentioned my message at all. I spent a lot of time at the library that day, really at the library.

I did come face to face with my father on Friday morning. He was angry.

"I had to cancel going to the mall this weekend for the watermelon slicing. What was I supposed to do? Try to hold the painted side away from the public? Keep smiling while I gazed at all those hideous wagging tongues? And anyway who'd want to eat a defaced watermelon? WM, Inc. composted them for fertilizer."

On Friday afternoon I had no classes, so I got home from school early. Daddy came in the back door shouting, "Dot...Dot...Dot..." Of course she wasn't home yet, but he went hobbling all the way down to their bedroom looking for her before he came back to my room.

"I've got the proof," he said, waving a piece of flowered cloth.

The police were not interested in investigating the watermelon caper. The melons were not owned by anyone since they were growing wild outside of private property, and the department had no jurisdiction on public land. The Bureau of Land Management, which was really in charge, had no sympathy for the illegal watermelons. WM, Inc. wanted to downplay the incident, as it revealed their attempt to harvest extra watermelons without paying for the acreage.

"Those D cops have no respect for law and order or the rights of a private citizen. Well, I went out to the watermelon farm myself and look what I found hanging like a flag on the south fence." He jiggled it in my face.

"Now what kind of a weirdo would wear a garment covered with ludicrous Hawaiian art, *in Arizona?* Ha. You don't have to answer. My vandaleous opponent has gone too far. He has a record, too. I checked him out. Arrested two years ago for defacing a beautiful Caterpillar tractor. Same M.O. as now. Obscene language. I will fully prosecute him of the law. Do you want to know what his real name is?"

"I know what his name is, but no law has been broken here. The watermelons in question were not on private land and their edibility was not endangered in any way. The company will never prosecute." I was shaking inside. "Besides, it wasn't Henry David Tarantula who painted the watermelons. It was me."

His red face turned white. It took him a while to say something.

"What about the writing on the hillside?"

"Yes."

"But you wrote an obscenity. Where did you learn that word? What would your mother say?"

"'Suck' is merely a statement of scientific fact. It is an accurate description of how all plants take up water. If someone has a dirty mind and misinterprets fact, it is not my responsibility."

"Cheese 'n crackers." His face was back to red again. "Why? Why in the world did you do it?"

"I'm opposed to watermelon farming here. It's bad for the environment. Neither our soil nor our water supply can sustain it." He wasn't listening.

"*You're* the one that's out to get me."

"No, it's that sleazy WM, Inc. that's out to get you." I was yelling back at him now. "All they care about is short-term profit, and you're the one that will be left holding the watermelon when the community runs out of drinking water."

"When your mother finds out about this, she'll...she'll... I better not tell her. But she'll find out somehow, she always finds out everything."

He turned to leave the room, slamming his fist into the door jamb on his way out. "You've turned against me."

"No, it's all politics. There's a lot of politics in biology."

"Cheese 'n crackers." He never turned me over to the D cops.

On Tuesday, Daddy won the election by a landslide. Henry David Tarantula got barely a smattering of votes, one of them mine. Daddy's face was on the front page of the newspaper again on Wednesday, but this time I was out of the picture.

GHOST SHIRT

I started with four rectangles of white cotton sheeting—two for the sleeves of the garment, one each for the front and back. I could feel Mrs. Sewing Pizzaroli's asshole begin to tighten in the netherworld. Tough to find plain white sheets. All the donated sheets at St. Vincent de Paul's and Salvation Army had some kind of stupid flowers on them. Why do people have to put flowers everywhere? Finally I got a plain white one begging at the back door of a motel from a person who couldn't speak English. Once I had my four rectangles cut out, I took the rest of the fabric to the all-night laundromat and dyed it in red Rit dye according to the "washing machine technique" outlined on the box. The box also said **Caution Eye Irritant,** *so I wore my motorcycle goggles. The washing machine said* **No Dyeing***, so I worked at midnight. It took four days to cut the fringe out of the red sheeting. I thought of slipping into the home economics building at Apache and copping time on a sewing machine to stitch the shirt together. But this is a holy garment, impenetrable by bullets or any weapons, its fringe the color of the sacred red paint of the Paiute messiah. I sew it all by hand, by candlelight.*

Chapter 16

GHOST SHIRT
"As fruits and leaves and the day itself acquire a bright tint just before they fall, so the year near its setting."
Henry David Thoreau, *"Autumnal Tints"*

After the Tuesday election, a Pacific storm hit the Oregon coast. It was immediately pushed southward by a trough of Arctic air, and it blazed a beeline for Arizona. By Friday, a gray ceiling settled over William and a blanket of invisibility spread across the San Miguels and Santa Isabellas. Summer was finally over.

After my morning classes, I went to the administration office at Apache College and had my transcripts sent to the University of Arizona. I also went to the bank. My parents would have to sign the paperwork for me to get a student loan. No need to ask them yet. I had a pile of application papers to fill out first. I set up my easel in the den. I painted clouds with just a thin gray line. Bright color was spread on the ground— red, yellow, gold, orange, pink, purple, turquoise, and fluorescent lime green leaves.

The doorbell rang. I could see why the Flower Shoppe mom was anxious to let Henry David go. He was a shocking sight with his frazzled hair, which was even more enlivened by the humidity, and the motorcycle goggles. He wore an over-sized calf-length Navy pea coat.

"Is your old man home?"

"No. Come in. Did you want to see him?"

"No. I came to ask if you would come to my un-victory party out at the cave tonight. We're all going to get bombed."

"Ummm, I can't borrow the truck tonight." I could just see myself asking Daddy to take his truck up to the Caves on a rainy night to illegally cavort with his opponent after doing my best to undermine his campaign platform.

"You could just come with me now."

They'd never miss me. Mom and Daddy had reveling of their own to do tonight. The Progress Party was holding a victory dinner that would surely last into the wee hours of the morning. Mike and Mack were roasting

Daddy. They'd better watch out for Mom. She drank only black coffee at parties.

"Okay. Just let me put away my paints."

Henry David followed me into the den. There were paintings lined up along the mantel of the fireplace, on the windowsills, stacked on the table and leaning against the wall. Mostly clouds. I closed up the paints and stepped into the kitchen to rinse the brushes while he stood humming at the easel, pondering my psychedelic autumn leaves.

"Why should leaves turn bright colors when they die?" he called out into the kitchen. "Why don't they just croak?"

"If it's a party, I should change my clothes," I yelled back.

I was wearing blue jeans with rips in both knees and a faded maroon sweatshirt with the cuffs and neck binding chopped off. In the past week, my clothing style had gone from sweet sixteen to gnarly hobo. Mom thought I was on drugs.

"If I ever find out you're smoking marijuana, I will cut you out of my will." She told me that one Saturday afternoon when I was pouring bleach on some brand new Levis.

"No need to change," he said. "Don't forget you'll be hanging out with the losers tonight. Bring your paints."

I threw the clean brushes in a shoe box containing my assorted tubes of acrylics, grabbed my trench coat, and left a note on the kitchen counter: "Gone to clean up my experiments."

I climbed into the flower truck and Henry David tightened up the motorcycle goggles.

"There's still pollen in here," he said.

I looked around and could imagine it circulating wildly in the back. There was also dust shooting up through a hole in the floor. As he pulled out of the driveway, he switched on the cat box, which broadcasted "*Meows*" from a speaker in the roof.

"This truck used to belong to the dogcatcher before the Flower Shoppe." He had to yell to be heard over the racket.

We crept down the street at 15 miles per hour, *meowing*. This was not the subtle getaway I had hoped for. The neighbors would be informing my parents. The cat box did entice one unrestrained dog. It was mottled black and gray and he shot out of a driveway at full yap. He came right alongside my window, one blue eye and one white eye, and Henry David swerved after him. We bumped up over the curb and chased him across a lawn—

there were no seatbelts in this truck—and almost slammed into a house as the dog skedaddled around the side yard.

"Flower men get bitten just as often as postmen," Henry David said.

"That was Mrs. Wilson's dog."

"Tell Mrs. Wilson to bite me."

Henry David backed out onto the street again. I switched off the cat box so we could talk, but neither one of us said anything. When we stopped at the last traffic light on the way out of town, Henry David rolled down his window and began beating on the steering wheel. Three hard smacks, then head out the window and explosion.

"*Ha-choo-y.*" He pulled himself back in the window. "If those nitwit Easterners insist upon polluting Arizona with their mulberry trees, oleanders and non-native flowers, I'm going to give them back in return all the germs I can sneeze out."

We jerked and squealed, Henry David's foot to the floor, up the mountain path, no concern whatever for the oil pan. He had one hand on the wheel and one pressing his goggles tight against his face. I was sneezing, too, as the dust cloud poured into the truck.

As we came to a halt at the cave's curbside parking, I finally asked the question.

"Did you make your pants?" These were the red corduroy/Levi crotch combo that he wore every time I'd seen him in pants. He told me the story as we sat in the truck outside the cave.

"I made them in sewing class at Apache."

"You took a sewing class?"

"Home economics is part of the agriculture department. I noticed the sewing machines on my way to classes, but they wouldn't let me use one unless I enrolled in sewing. Mrs. Sewing Pizzaroli—I can't remember her real name—with a gray bun tried to make me make an apron. I made these pants instead."

"What did Mrs. Pizzaroli think of the pants?"

"She stuck me with a pin."

Henry David got out and went into the cave, leaving me sitting there in the truck.

"Autumn leaves are a gift." I said it to myself.

Up here in the Santa Isabella foothills, we were closer to the clouds. They curled and licked their way down the canyons. The air was heavy and the smell of creosote wafted across the desert like a large, lazy woman. Out of the cave came the tinkling of piano music. I picked up my box of art supplies and followed it in.

I was stunned by the power of the artificial sun I had created months ago, now studded with lit candles that were nestled into the hollows and irregularities of the cave wall. Also surprising was the presence of another woman who sat in the natural light beneath the window, hovering over a simmering, spicy cookpot. She had black, straight hair, even longer than mine, a dark complexion, and wore a long, pale orange sari-like dress. She did not acknowledge my presence, nor did Henry David introduce her.

"Did you want me to paint something?" I yelled over the music. Henry David raised a finger in the direction of a white object that swayed ever so slightly beneath the fishnets. It looked like the sagging ghost of a scarecrow. Moving closer I saw that it was an article of clothing, a shirt, a magnificent shirt I realized, as I carefully removed it from a hook on the fishnet.

It was made of soft white cotton, long sleeved with a deep "V" in the front. Its most stunning feature was its fringe. This was dark-colored and luxuriously thick, about four inches long, encircling the neck and cuffs. It also hung in foot-long clumps from the seams at the elbows, underarms and shoulders. Taking the shirt into the light, I saw that the fringe was bright red. Feathers were tied in clusters of three and attached along the outside of the arms. Black feathers, probably from a raven, and the unmistakable gray, black and white feathers of mourning doves.

"This shirt is amazing," I said, "You want me to paint on this?"

Henry David sprang from his stool, grabbing a book from a stack on the top of the piano. He brought it over to me, and I could see by its markings that it was from the library. Flipping to a bookmark, he ripped out a page and dropped the book on the floor.

"This is what I want." He flicked his Bic lighter and showed me a photo of a similar shirt, but with animals painted on it. There were pairs of crows on the front, along with a tortoise and some symbols, and a bison on each sleeve. "I want the black birds for sure and this one symbol that looks like a Maltese cross. It represents the morning star. You can paint whatever you like on the rest."

"You just ripped up a library book," I called after him as he walked out of the cave.

The exotic-looking woman was now sitting against the wall, her eyes closed, swaying and dipping to the echo of the music. She hadn't said a word since I had come in, and I began to wonder, given her appearance, if she spoke English. I sat down under the wall of candles and studied the torn page. The header carried the book title: *The Ghost-Dance Religion and the Sioux Outbreak of 1890*. The photo caption said "Arapaho Ghost Dance shirt."

He was certainly fixated on ghosts. The Ghost Dance was the final hope and hurrah of the Plains Indian culture, a blast of color before their grim confinement to the Reservation. I had read that the Ghost Dance had originated in the White Mountains of Arizona, not actually on the Plains.

I started with two black birds, painting them high on the chest. I made them larger than in the photo, not crows but ravens. I painted a fluorescent turquoise Maltese cross at the lower right near the shirttail. It would glow in the dark like the morning star. Lower left I put a coiling snake with yellow, orange and black stripes. Center front I painted a giant hairy tarantula with red eyes.

On the sleeves I chose desert animals instead of the bison. A lime green jackrabbit on one side and a purple javelina on the other. While I was waiting for the front to dry, I did a little more work on the sleeves, painting a few zigzags of lightning and the three-toed tracks of birds.

The photo didn't show the back of the shirt. Henry David had disappeared and the woman seemed to be asleep. I carefully turned the shirt face down. Beneath the fringe, I lined the neck with yellow stars and placed a bright orange crescent moon between the shoulder blades. I clustered more black birds along the sides. In the lower back center, I painted a large red wolf. He stood on his hind legs as if dancing to Henry David's insane music, waving his front legs like arms. He, too, was covered with the zigzags of lightning and the black tracks of birds. His eye was a yellow star, and more stars cascaded out of his mouth and then upward to join the moon. He might have been eating stars or howling stars. I put my paints away without cleaning the brushes and stormed outside looking for Henry David. He was lying under the creosote bush.

"So, who's your girlfriend?"

"What are you talking about?" He stood up and gave me that low laugh.

"Who's the woman in the cave? Why didn't you introduce us?"

He brushed it off. "That's Mira. She has some deep kharma she is trying to work out right now. She's very mellow."

Mira's therapy seemed to involve Henry David's physique. She slithered up behind him and entwined herself under his arms and around his chest. Her hair hung almost to her knees. We still didn't speak to each other. I noticed she had a black dot painted just above her eyebrows in the center of her forehead, and at that moment Bruce "the Snake" Smith arrived.

Bruce was better heeled, or better tread, than what I expected of a sometimes cave dweller. He had a black, highly polished Japanese truck with a maroon coiled snake decal in the center of the hood. The tires were big enough for a one-ton flatbed. They protruded out of the wheel wells with a super toothy tread that climbed up the desert to the cave, stereo bass booming, with no need for a road.

Bruce's sex appeal was all in his truck. What dropped out of the cab was a small, skinny, light-colored guy with oversized black plastic-framed glasses. With high-speed energy, he began unloading the back—various stereo speakers, instrument boxes, a set of drums and a keg of beer. Henry David didn't introduce me to Bruce either. Bruce himself was very polite.

"You must be Virginia," he said. "I'm Bruce Smith, and I really like your painting in the cave. May I get you a glass of beer?"

He tapped the keg, which had been placed under the large creosote, gave it a couple of pumps and presented me with a large plastic glass of mostly foam, for which he apologized.

"The foam's my favorite part," I told him.

As more trucks drove up the hill, I slipped down the slope to the pecan tree and my abandoned plot. The garlic stems had curled into full circles signifying that it was time to harvest. The African daisies had never gotten very tall but had bloomed well after all. I had missed the glory. What was left were dried brown heads still packed with seeds. I plucked a few, dropping them into the pocket of my jeans. Clementine was in a high branch of the tree. Her hair was a mess and her ears were tucked down into her collar. She sat stubbornly facing east as the sun was heading west.

"One of your ancestors probably planted this tree," I said to the bird. "Probably flew all the way here from the Tumacacori Mission with a mouthful of pecans to hide."

She didn't respond.

"You know, Clementine, he's really not right for you. His heart is like a rock and he doesn't care about anybody. You need to find yourself a fuzzy black bird with a big sense of humor who won't throw things at you. How about a little money? Won't that cheer you up?"

I took my emergency phone money—five shiny dimes—out of my right tennis shoe and put them on the dirt under the tree. Clementine flew right down, but she didn't pick them up immediately. She paced and murmured in the forsaken plot. I sipped my beer foam and murmured back.

Up at the cave, the music started. Electric guitar, drums and no piano, thank goodness. Mira came down the hill with a fresh glass of beer for me, no foam this time, and an oblong box tucked under her arm. Clementine squawked, put all the dimes in her mouth, and flew away.

"Would you like to play a game of Scrabble?" Mira asked in perfect English. Actually, Scrabble was my favorite game. Cynthia hadn't been able to beat me since I was 10 years old. We spread out under the tree and went at it like tigers. Mira had wide lips darkened with a brownish stain and glowing brown eyes. Here eyebrows were thicker than mine and shapelier. She annihilated me. I wondered if it was the beer. I had finished the second glass.

"What's your relationship with Henry David?" I asked Mira. That definitely was a response to the second glass.

"He lets me stay at the cave. I needed some time away from my husband and two-year-old daughter. We are lovers, of course. It's helping me straighten out my head." Judging from her Scrabble, I couldn't see anything the matter with her head.

"How sweet of him."

"He's so philosophical."

I had to go pee. I walked about a quarter of a mile before I found a bush that suited me, then wound my way back up to the party, avoiding the pecan and hoping Mira would keep off my plot.

Many more people had arrived along with another keg. Henry David hadn't gathered enough votes in the election to have this many disappointed supporters, but word of a party travels fast on a campus and he had attracted a college crowd. Most probably had never heard of Henry David, and they certainly didn't know their way around a cactus, judging from their footwear. The clouds had been gray all day long. At sunset they turned indigo blue then darkened to black night.

Bruce tapped away at the drums on the front porch of the cave, and Henry David gyrated Mick Jagger-style without any singing, pulling out his harmonica when the mood hit him. Mustache Mike was the real musician. When the rest of the group petered out, Mustache put away his electric guitar, sat on a folding chair in the headlights of Bruce's truck with a beat-up acoustical guitar, and sang Bob Dylan for an hour. He had a thick, straight mane of dark hair that hung almost to his shoulders and a heavy mustache like an Earp brother. Clementine would really go for him. I was sitting just outside the circle of light from the truck, and Bruce brought me another beer and an aluminum foil pie plate filled with curried rice, broccoli and chicken. I ate with my fingers. Mira was a great cook.

"Don't you live in a cave, too?" I asked Bruce when he sat down next to me on the ground.

"No, I messed around with that for about a week, but my father had a fit. I'm living in a frat house at the U of A now." I might have guessed by his short haircut and leather shoes. I recalled the ragged clothes I was wearing beneath my trench coat. The sky was still heavy, but there was no movement. The clouds held the warm air close to the earth. The food was gone, but the beer flowed. Someone switched on a stereo. Bruce asked me to dance, and since Henry David and Mira were wrapped around each other, barely moving during a fast rock song, I said yes. Bruce was a great dancer, a showman. The next song was slow and Bruce tucked his arms inside my trench coat and held me close, his head resting on my shoulder. Henry David had slipped away and Mira was swaying by herself.

"I have to get some more beer," I said.

I wanted to get away from Bruce and find Henry David. After filling my glass, I found him off by himself on a rock sucking on a toilet paper roll with a joint sticking vertically out of the top. He had shed the huge pea coat and was now bare chested. He obviously had been into my paints. There was a black tarantula painted on his chest. He held the smoke in his lungs for a moment then burst into a fit of coughing.

When he recovered, he didn't offer me any of the smoke. Instead, he handed me a twig. Attached were three feathers—one raven, two dove.

"You like Bruce more than you like me," he said. "Bruce is a snake," and he walked away and into the cave.

At least I had taken time to comb my hair before I had come to this party. I had plaited two long braids, which were perfect for the feathers. I wove the twig into one side of my hair. In a few moments Henry David emerged from his front doorway wearing the ghost shirt.

"Oh, so now you want to be Crazy Horse?" I charged. "Who *are* you?"

Without a word to me, Henry David stood in the spotlight of the truck beams, arms out to the side, displaying the fringe of the shirt like a strutting raven. He commandeered the attention of the entire party. All chatter and laughter suddenly ceased.

"Follow me to the river," he yelled. He led the way to the arroyo, hardly a river, with a flashlight, and a couple of guys made sure a keg came, too. I stayed up top on the limestone porch for a while and drank my beer, but my lonely reverie was soon disturbed by the sound of wild sex going on inside the cave. I joined the crowd down the hill.

Chapter 17

THE ROAST

"You swallowed it, you drank it
Beautifully drunk, beautifully dizzy
You didn't keep me from the good talk."
Tohono O'odham Seating Speech

You do not mess with Dot. After George's four years in office, you'd think his buddies would realize this. But Mike and Mack continued on in an uninterrupted course of shooting themselves in the foot.

The victory dinner for the Progress Party was held at The Bistro, the most expensive restaurant in town, owned by none other than Town Councilman Mike Sherwood. Like its owner, it was more flash than substance. At least that was Dot's opinion. George didn't have a clue. The lights were kept low and the liquor was served promptly, so it wasn't obvious that the dark wood was cardboard trailer paneling, the black chairs were plastic, and the white tablecloths covered rickety, formica-topped, metal-legged furniture out of a breakfast cafe. Elegantly named entrees and steep prices added to the illusion.

Tonight's menu consisted of the usual Garden Delight salad—a wedge of iceberg lettuce topped with a slather of French dressing. The main course was Medallions of Beef, actually chunks of sirloin sprinkled early that morning with meat tenderizer, lying with baby carrots in a bed of packaged gravy, and Golden Baked Potatoes, just russets wrapped in gold aluminum foil. No one knew where Mike got that gold foil. It was like his secret ingredient, and it really dressed up a dinner.

By accident, Mike had stumbled upon another magic formula that truly made his restaurant a success: Cece Potter. He had begrudgingly hired Cece seven years ago as a server when applicants were scarce. He didn't like her style—skinny, tight page-boy hair, forty-ish. He felt young and sexy would bring in more business. Was he ever wrong. Seven years later, Cece still looked exactly the same and, as head waitress, she ran the dining room with tight-assed efficiency. The wait staff wore white blouses and black skirts that covered their knees, and they kept white napkins neatly draped over their left forearms.

Without Cece, Dot could never have survived an occasion like a cash bar. She retreated to Cece's corner, a lighted alcove just off the dining room, where Cece could keep an eagle eye on customers and staff while smoking like a chimney. Cece and Dot sipped black coffee. Cece never raised a droplet of alcohol near her thin lips after wrestling for 20 years with an alcoholic husband who dropped dead on her just before she got the Bistro job. Cece and Dot had been in high school together and these chats in the smoky corner during political dinners were the only times either one of them ever giggled.

By the time the politicos sat down to the iceberg lettuce, George was slightly slurring with champagne. His navy blue suit was rumpled around the pockets and his striped tie had picked up a zigzag. Dot was buzzing with caffeine, and she still had not removed her rose red coat with the black velvet collar.

"Dottie girl, oh Dottie girl, oh won't you marry up with me," George sang not far under his breath in her right ear as he helped her with the coat. Dottie dug her right stiletto heel into his left foot.

Yowl.

"Next time it'll be your right foot." She plastered on a smile as she took her seat at the head table, thankful for all the tenderizer on the meat as she ate her meal facing the other diners, pretending an animated conversation with her husband.

"Mumbo jumbo," she said leaning toward him demurely.

"Dumbo bumbo." He tried unsuccessfully to raise his eyebrow.

"An astute observation," she returned as Mike stood up to begin the ceremonies.

"Victory is not a big enough word." Mike huffed and puffed. "We burned their butts. It was a conflagration. Or, as George would say, a conflabberation."

The room rocked with laughter, only George not getting the joke. Dot bent her spoon in half.

"I know you'll want to hear a few victory words from the big man, the old watermelon kisser himself, George, P as in Progress, Stone."

The audience was on its tipsy legs applauding. George, always slow to transition from chair to feet, was still fishing in his inside coat pocket for the note cards with his speech. Meanwhile, Mike and a spotlight borrowed from the theater company were both pointing in the opposite direction—away from George, toward the kitchen. Bursting through the swinging door came Mike's Town Council sidekick Mack. Mack, himself bald as a billiard ball, wore an unruly wig with long muttonchop sideburns that must have been come with a Teddy Roosevelt costume. His suit, however, was more in the style of Liberace. Rhinestone-studded, royal blue velvet.

The diners fell back into their chairs laughing as Mack limped and staggered over to the podium at the head table. After four martinis, it wasn't all an act. Dot took a hard pull from her coffee cup.

"I've always enjoyed playing with fire," Mack said.

That was the signal for Mike to start the film that was projected on the white wall behind Mack. The video started with clips from Channel 4 News of Chief George in full turnout in front of various William burning buildings. He was agile as a wolf in those days, eyes blazing, firing commands into the radio, leaping from red trucks and silver ladders, furiously pawing hoses. At least they'd had the decency to exclude any footage of the Hardware fire. Still, tears poured down Dot's cheeks.

"But now in my maturity, I'm a little more relaxed," Mack commented. There stood George at the front door of his own house in undershirt and paisley shorts, hair as disheveled as Mack's wig.

Mack's drunken narration continued over the whistles and hoots. "And for the sake of progress and the benefit of the community, I have devoted myself to kissing watermelons." The cameraman hiding in the tree well that night after the press conference had recorded the scene perfectly, the voluptuous Millie trying to barge into the Stone home. Running the film backwards made it look like George was making a face plant on Millie's watermelons. The clip was run backwards and forwards, backwards and forwards for at least ten nauseating seconds, neither Dot nor George breathing, the rest of the audience uproarious.

Finally, the scene changed to a close-up of the younger George, beaming into a news camera, reciting his famous adage, "The best way to stop a fire is with a brick wall."

Immediately Dot's face flashed on screen. The cameraman hadn't been completely stupefied by the threatened violence, because there she was in her fire engine red bathrobe, hair a-swirl, shotgun in hands, snarl set like concrete. Mike and Mack were the only idiots laughing. Dot's chair scraped across the floor and she stormed to the podium, sobering Mack instantly with stiletto pressure to his instep.

"And don't you forget it," she blasted into the microphone.

The dance band leader was smart enough to intervene with a victory tune, "Seventy-six trombones..."

FROM THE JOURNAL OF HENRY DAVID TARANTULA

THE VIRGIN

She must be a virgin. She is the dumbest chick I have ever seen. Wearing those stupid round sunglasses with silver lenses painted with pink and blue bubbles. What is she, a clown? I looked into those glasses and saw myself. I tore them off her. Her eyes are pond blue. Reflective. Mirroring the colors of her surroundings. I looked into them and saw myself. Infuriating. She has a small chin and with a dimple in it. Flouncing lace and penetrating questions. I felt off-balance. I poured out my thoughts. She must be a virgin. A white dress. Black hair tied in a knot. Soft, beyond the control of reason. A crescendo of heat. What is the point of virginity? She is like a desert lake surrounded by poisonous green gypsum hills, the water lavender silver. What was she writing in that notebook? Challenging my acidic rationality. No flowers can survive. What economy is there in beauty?

Chapter 18

GHOST DANCE

"When one burns one's bridges, what a very nice fire it makes."
Dylan Thomas

Henry David had dragged underbrush from around the desert and created a huge pile in the dry creek bed. He topped the pile with a decaying cow's leg. Now he poured on a partial can of yellow automotive paint and tossed in a match. There was a spattering and up shot two columns, one a straight yellow flame and beside it a spiral of white steam. The two intermingled and separated and chased each other around the pile until all the brush had ignited.

Henry David took a handful of fine silt from the arroyo, washed his hands in it and threw it over his head. Then he joined hands with the two people adjacent to him. Bruce and Mustache seemed to be familiar with the ritual and did the same, Bruce taking my hand, entwining my fingers. The rest of the partiers caught on and soon we formed a big ring around the bonfire. Except for Mira, who was dancing alone outside the circle like an Indian Isadora Duncan, her sheer sari spiraling like the steam. She had a small conga drum tucked under one arm and a round-headed mallet with which she beat a low, uneven rhythm to accompany her movement.

Henry David stepped to the left, sliding his foot through the dirt, then scuffed his right foot along to meet it. The circle began moving slowly in a clockwise rotation, fine, flour-like dust rising around our knees. Mira's drumming became louder and stronger. She settled into a four-beat measure, accent on the first.

BOOM, boom, boom, boom. BOOM, boom, boom, boom.

The wind kicked up and we were enveloped in dust, almost hidden from each other, the dancing becoming more intense, our arms swinging high and bodies swaying. The fire burned deep red inside and around the perimeter it was as warm as summer, even when cold raindrops began pounding on our heads.

"*Ba nina' nina' ta, ni' taba na.*" Henry David sang in shrill falsetto. "*Nana' nina' hu'hu.*" He seemed to have finally found tone, words and rhythm that perfectly communicated his turbulent soul, though I still couldn't understand him.

"He'e'e'e' Ih! Ih!"

BOOM, *boom, boom, boom.* BOOM, *boom, boom, boom.*

"The raven has called me." Henry David was yelling.

Again, "The raven has called me, when the raven came for me, when the raven came for me, I heard him, I heard him."

I remembered my nightmare. I began having it at about four years old and it recurred until long after I was in school. There was dust in the air, a dust devil whipping in circles and stinging my legs, dark swirling dust with a red light in the center and drumming, drumming. As the light came closer, I could see it was a fire. I was in a cave and there were bare feet around a campfire. It was the bare feet that scared me, and I would wake up screaming for my father. He would bring me a glass of water and I would lie back down, the long bones in my legs aching and aching.

The rest of the crowd seemed to interpret it more as a Bacchanalian celebration. Revelers picked up the *"He'e'e'e' Ih! Ih!"* and chanted along. They laughed and shouted and gyrated till a few of them fell over. They thought it was really funny when Henry David began throwing his campaign leaflets into the burn. First it was the various flyers he had strewn about on lawns. Then came his large tarantula campaign sign that once stood in Armory Park. The rain pounded down on us and the fire sizzled.

Next came Henry David's books. The crowd howled as he called out their titles and tossed them in the fire, one after another: His political science texts, his agriculture books, the county building regulations, National Uniform Fire Code, his sewing machine instructions. I screamed each time but was drowned out in the prevailing hilarity and the fury of the fire. My hands were locked by Bruce on one side and some reeling oaf on the other, who dragged me along like a rag doll in their frenzied movements.

"*Walden.*" Henry David shouted, "*Walden.*" He threw *Walden* into the flames.

"No No No No No." I screamed it again and again. I jerked away from the circle of dancers and lurched after *Walden* into the fire.

If my hair and face hadn't been soaking wet and Bruce hadn't reacted so fast, I might have been burned or at least singed. Bruce jerked me backwards and rolled me in the sand. Then Henry David was in my face shouting.

"You stupid virgin."

Shoot him. I wanted to shoot him. I tried to slap him, but the impact I managed to make with his face was such a light touch he burst out laughing. I pulled myself to my knees, grabbed rocks and started hurling them. He walked away and I don't think I even hit him once.

I could hear tittering around the fire about a stupid virgin. I straightened up and backed into the dark. Henry David stood silhouetted against the flames, the wide shoulders and fluttering fringe of his ghost shirt, the round tangle of his hair. He was laughing and howling and then burst into a fit of coughing.

The clouds had blown apart and there was a slightly waning moon and billions of stars. The lights of the city shone below me and I headed toward them, figuring the arroyo would take me there. I had given all my money to Clementine, so I couldn't even make a phone call once I got to the edge of town, but I really didn't know who to call anyway. The alcohol and adrenalin were wearing off and I was starting to shiver.

I hadn't gotten very far when Bruce came after me in his truck. He wrapped Henry David's long pea coat around my shoulders, and it took a tremendous amount of pulling on my part and pushing on his to get me all the way up into the cab. I immediately vomited on the dashboard. He patiently mopped it up with a roll of paper towels he had stored behind the seat. Throwing the smeared towels out the window, he turned the heater on full blast and took me home.

"Why does he treat me so badly?" I asked Bruce. I also wondered why Bruce treated me so well, even after I threw up in his truck. But Bruce didn't venture an opinion, just quietly set me off at my doorstep. I slipped in through the kitchen. My parents were not even home yet.

FROM THE JOURNAL OF HENRY DAVID TARANTULA

When the music seizes me, it courses down my arms and legs, grabs my spine and shakes me like a rattle. It bangs inside my head like a metal spoon on the lid of a garbage can. Sweat leaks out of my scalp until my hair sticks together in greasy clumps. Stars erupt in the back of my eyes. I can't sing, so I shout, my voice as ragged as Rod Stewart's. I can't dance, so I reel and lurch and thrash about. That is my whole portion with the rock band called Dirt.

Mustache Mike is our only musician. He's a genius, but he's no showman. He dresses in army fatigues and hunches over his Fender Stratocaster, oblivious to all except the intricate electronic battlefield of notes he creates in one run after another. His music is a collision of tinkling celestial spheres and the bubbling murky pool from which life began.

Bruce the Snake is our manager and drummer. He is all show. He pounds a relentless beat on a shiny set of drums and wears silk shirts with big sleeves. He books us for grunge engagements, parties where there's lots of dope and alcohol and they want us to play all night. Mustache is the only one who can go all night.

I envisioned a trumpet. Or a tuba. Just a few keys, big noise, it's all in the lip. To add to the act, Bruce the Snake drove me to the Ragtime Store in Tucson, the only place in the yellow pages that advertised used musical instruments. It was on a dilapidated downtown back street, a big store on the corner, with some old furniture strewn about in the alley behind and a crapped-out piano on the front porch. Advertising was painted in white script on the front windows, most items $99.99. Owner was a prick.

"How much money you got?"

"Fifteen dollars."

He slapped a harmonica on the table and darted off to another customer. The silver-plated sides were as polished as a mirror. The wooden mouthpiece was bruised but bright red. It lay inside a box lined with black velvet though much of the fuzzy nap had worn off.

Bruce the Snake was hissing. "Man, you gonna let him get away with that kind of disrespect? Hey," he hollered after the storekeeper. "HEY."

I looked up at the ceiling and stared at the fan as it lugubriously circled, its big paddles carrying swaths of spider webs. I took out fifteen dollars, laid it on the table and pocketed the harmonica. Bruce followed me out of the store protesting.

"I can't believe you just paid fifteen bucks for a filthy harmonica."

"We're also taking the piano."

Chapter 19

THE PIANO
"Living much out of doors, in the sun and wind, will no doubt produce a certain roughness of character."
Henry David Thoreau, *"Walking"*

Just three days later I received a package in the mail. It was a charred copy of Henry David Thoreau's *Walden.* Inside was a note scrawled on crumpled paper that looked like it had been out in the rain. It was in that odd script that ran backwards across the page: "Virginia, I'm leaving the cave. Please take my piano."

On Sunday morning, Daddy and Everett, with me squashed in between straddling the gear shift, bounded up the rocky road to Henry David's cave in the bright blue International. We pulled a small, low trailer for hauling the piano.

"Cheese 'n crackers," Daddy repeated at every chuckhole. "How can anyone live up such a rocky undulation so far removed from the necessary conveniences?"

I didn't mention that he might try to go through the holes more slowly. It had been a calculated risk asking him to help me in the first place. When I had finally ventured the request, he was sitting on an overturned bucket behind the house amid the broken remains of a yellow brick wall.

"People don't ask me to build much anymore," he said, "but they're always anxious for me to tear things down." He was cleaning the old mortar off each brick with a geologist's hammer and stacking them in neat piles, two by two in alternating directions for stability. His hands were swollen and hard. He wore an un-ironed flannel shirt for a jacket with only the middle two buttons fastened and a light blue cotton hat that said "Disneyland." Mom obviously hadn't laid out his clothes that morning.

"Where'd you get the yellow bricks?"

"It's part of the old Shell gas station down by the college. They're putting in some kind of fast-food place. Hired some big outfit from Tucson to build it and they just bulldozed the gas station. They were going to take the whole pile to the landfill, but I talked the foreman into just moving it to the corner of the lot instead. I'm using the Waldon to haul it away a little at a time. It'll save their company a lot of work and a big dumping fee, and I'm recycling all these beautiful bricks."

"Going to build the yellow brick road?"

"No, but when I saw these yellow bricks, I knew they were meant for me. I have an idea, but nothing to say out loud yet. I just need to beat out the details here on the brick pile for a few weeks and then maybe I'll mention it to your mother."

"Henry David Tarantula wants to give me his piano."

If it hadn't been for the glorious nature of his re-election, the clearing of the weather, which had reduced the pain in his metal heel, and the windfall of the bricks, I don't think I would have had a prayer. Even so, his merry mood receded under a black cloud.

"Cheese 'n crackers." He mumbled that under his breath. "Don't tell me he keeps a piano in his cave."

"Yes, but he's moved out of the cave now and he wants me to come get the piano."

"How do you know where this cave is?"

"Actually, I stumbled upon it while I was working on my science project. I was testing the soils in that area."

"Horse feathers."

I let it simmer. I suspected Daddy would have a strong ulterior motive—finding out the exact location of the Caves. Sure enough, on Sunday morning he was ready to go and had coerced my annoying brother-in-law Everett into going along, too.

Everett didn't say a word in the truck. His feet were braced against the floorboards, his arms tightly clenched across his chest and his lips a livid line. It turned out that saying "I do" to Cynthia had some weekend implications with respect to Daddy. To make it worse, Daddy's projects always started at 6 o'clock in the morning. It was barely light outside.

I also had my arms crossed and feet braced, determined not to be shaken loose from my position in the truck. About halfway up the barely visible road, Daddy slammed over a rock so hard that, even with my seatbelt on, my head banged into the ceiling of the cab. He finally slowed down.

Tatters of the storm still clung to the Santa Isabella Mountains. The cave seemed a hundred years deserted, not just a week, the saguaro at the door so wizened, the creosote in the front yard dilapidated. It was cold and my blackened trench coat was secretly at the dry cleaners. I wore Henry

David's Navy pea coat. It hung to my ankles and was about a foot too wide at the shoulders, the arms completely hiding my hands.

"Where'd you get that disgusting coat?" Everett finally said something. "It smells like smoke and goat piss."

"Hey, watch your language there, son."

I held back as the two men entered the cave. Daddy carried a magnum spotlight.

"Son of a bee." I didn't know whether he had flashed on the fluorescent stars, the fishing nets, the yellow sunbeams, or the tower of beer cans. I hiked down to my old plot under the pecan tree. No Clementine. The garlic plants lay prostrate in the dirt. I noticed some scratching on the trunk of the tree. Peering closer, the letters were clear: CLEM. Also, there was an arrow with long feathers on the shaft. I had my Swiss army knife, of course, and I carved my own message. It was hard work in the tough old wood.

"This piano is a piece of junk." That was Everett yelling.

I wove my way around the arroyo. There was a ring of fire-cracked rocks streaked with black lines like spiders with long twisting legs. Within the ring was a small pile of ashes, little bits of burned paper, and a few large cow bones. Partly buried in the dirt just outside the firepit, I saw three feathers tied to a twig, my twig. I had forgotten. It must have fallen out of my hair during the ghost dance. I blew off the dust and tucked it back into my braid. A wind started up at the top of the hill, thrashed its way through the bushes, and nudged me sideways. Henry David's coat was heavy and unwieldy, but I could feel its power. I spread it open like a cape, turned my back to the wind, and practically flew down the arroyo.

"Cheese 'n crackers" came down from the cave as they struggled with the piano. I tore around the desert with dark wings.

The trip home dragging the loaded trailer through the desert was painfully slow and stubbornly quiet. Everett had his eyes clenched shut pretending to be asleep, his head thumping the window with each rut. Daddy never said a word until we pulled into the driveway.

"I'll go back for all those beer cans some other time."

Mom took one look at the piano and said, "I won't have that filthy thing in my house." Daddy stored it in his workshop under a tarp.

Mom never pursued the watermelons. Under normal circumstances she would have nailed the culprit and ground her up in a pulp machine, but right now she was pre-occupied with the upcoming arrival of Cynthia's baby. With barely four months left before the expected delivery date, Mom was spending weekends shopping and helping Cynthia decorate the "nursery." Uncertain as to the sex of the baby, every decision took a great deal of consideration. They were several weeks alone figuring out what color to paint the walls. A combination of pink and blue (could it cause gender confusion?), aqua (nothing would go with it), eggshell yellow (if the baby were jaundiced, he/she might look worse). Everett was smart enough to stay out of it and Daddy learned quickly.

White. They finally decided on white because they could easily paint over it if they changed their minds later. Daddy did the paint job. Winnie the Pooh was the room's "theme," which seemed to be a much easier decision for them than the background color. Soon there was a crib, dresser, changing table, rocking chair, musical mobiles, a toy box, an Eeyore lamp, a giant Winnie, and a bookshelf with Winnie the Pooh books, dolls and puppets. Then they started filling up the dresser and the toy box. Next they created lists for the upcoming (in two months) baby shower. Mom said at eight months she would start stocking their freezer so Cynthia wouldn't have to cook for a while. Cynthia was still vomiting, and she looked like she swallowed a field of Sugar Daddies.

I chose one of Mom's preoccupied moments to introduce the subject of transferring to the University in Tucson in January. It wasn't much of an argument.

"How do you plan to pay for it?"

"I'm going to apply for a student loan if you will sign the papers."

"Fine. That will teach you something about spending money. Just don't expect me to help you pick out a wardrobe. I'm too busy."

Clothes were very low on my list of priorities. Two pairs of jeans, two black turtlenecks, sweatpants, a handful of T-shirts and the pea coat would get me through the winter. I wasn't exactly going to join a sorority. There was no offer of a vehicle, but once I got there, my bicycle would be fine. I shopped for a new notebook at Ben Franklin's and found a blank composition book covered with thick drawing paper and stamped with autumn leaves. I bought a pack of ten medium point black Bic pens and a small box of colored pencils. I packed the science kit and *Walden* and was ready to go by December first though the semester didn't start until mid-January.

In the evenings I worked in the den at my easel. Usually I started by blacking out the previous night's painting and starting again. I could never get it as good as the original on the ghost shirt. Over and over I painted a red wolf with white lightning on his sides. The yellow moon shone behind his head and his eyes were stars. There were etchings, like bird tracks, on the animal's face and back.

"Forget your dreams, Virginia," Mom said to me when she first saw it.

Tonight Daddy was at his usual place on the couch by the fireplace playing Solitaire on the coffee table at his knees. His deck of cards was old, each card thick and brittle, stiff like his own hands and salted with the sticky residue of beer nuts. There were rings on the table from his glasses of highly sweetened iced tea. The table itself was a little unbalanced, with one slightly shorter leg, and it moved with the game.

"Come on, come on," Daddy commanded the cards as he struggled to get them unstuck from each other.

"Goddamn sonofabitch," he exclaimed when he now couldn't come up with the two of spades for his ace, which had earlier brought a hoot and holler. He fanned through the deck again, three cards at a time, slamming the cards on the table. Finally stumped, he threw down the whole deck. Then suddenly delighted, he said, "Well, if you're going to be in here, Virginia, let's light a fire."

I had overheard Mom breaking the news to Daddy a few weeks ago.

"She needs to go, Darling."

Daddy was crying. "She's my baby. Why can't she stay here one more semester like Cynthia?"

"She's vandalized the ceiling in her own bedroom and have you seen her latest painting? She's certainly out of the pastel stage and she needs to forget about Henry David Tarantula."

Daddy worked well on his knees and crumpled up some newspaper and stacked on some small pieces of scrap wood from the cardboard box beside the fireplace. Once he got the newspaper lit, he replaced the screen, and sidled back onto the couch. He began shuffling cards for a new game, but his attention was held by the fire as the newspaper flared quickly, the flames licked around the chunks of one-by and two-by-fours and then jumped ecstatically to a plate-sized disk of plywood. The fire was soon breathing hard and the warmth reddened my father's face and started to touch my bare ankles.

In a low, slow, deep voice—one I had never heard before from my father—in a poetry I had never imagined in him, he said, "Fire so sweet at its birth, so voracious in its progress, so unmerciful in its consummation." Was he speaking to me? His gaze was still entranced by the fire. I paused in my painting, brush in mid-air, and waited in careful silence, not wanting to disturb the moment. He didn't mess up a single word.

"I never hesitated," he continued. "I was so angry at the builder of the Hardware who put three roofs on a fire trap with no windows in the upper story let alone a sprinkler system, to say nothing of the arsonist who jeopardized the life of a young fireman with a black-haired seven-year-old daughter and a wife whose name was also Dorothy." He finally took a breath. "I shrieked like an Apache, bounded across the roof, grabbed Lane by the collar, jerked him out of the flaming hole and flung him at the belayers." Daddy was jerking and flinging at the air.

"Then I couldn't catch my balance," his hands, still holding the cards, were weaving above his head now, "couldn't get back to the ladder, the roof collapsed under my feet." He stopped waving. "In that prolonged split second I could see three floors down into the concrete basement. There was black smoke flowing like oil and then yellow fire leaping toward me. Falling meant not only death but hell." Still speaking to the fire, he said, "It was the wind that saved me. The howling updraft created by the hole in the roof. It lifted me with it. I threw myself toward the alleyway and I ran. I ran on the wind toward the alleyway, and even after the wind dropped me, I kept running, running. I remembered it was my birthday."

As our own fire noisily sparked and flared in a rainbow of yellows, oranges and red, Daddy dropped his cards back on the table and drew a final, surprising conclusion. "Love is a purifying fire." That remark jolted him out of his reverie. "Dot, Dot, Dot…" he yelled. Instantly, I heard the kitchen chair screech—my mother was watching her small television at the kitchen counter—and she scuffed into the den in her puffy backless house slippers.

"Is it time for bed yet?" he asked.

"Yes, Darling, I'll turn off the TV."

I wondered if Daddy had ever told the whole story to Mom. I tried to get back to work on the painting, but I mostly just stared at it until the fire died out. Besides some lackadaisical work on my Apache College classes and disinterested participation in the holidays, there was little more for me to do but wait for my new journey to begin.

Chapter 20

THE JOURNEY
"We should go forth on the shortest walk, perchance, in the spirit of undying adventure, never to return . . ."
Henry David Thoreau, *"Walking"*

Trap came out of the trees and into the Animas Valley of New Mexico, and he ran for the sheer pleasure of the grass. He threw a stick and chased it, then rolled over and over scratching himself in the green roughage. He stayed on his back gazing up at the blue and snoozed a bit.

Four mallards awakened the black wolf as they made a quacking descent into the nearby Indian Creek. Immediately alert and on his belly, Trap slithered toward the water. About fifty feet away he stopped. A trickster at heart, he took a couple of deep breaths and launched himself straight up in the air. The mallards, at the sight of a splayed legged hairy canine, ran on the water and took to the skies. Trap trotted to the pool, splashed in, cavorted in circles, lapped a long drink and stood immersed to his chest as the water gently played around him. It had been a long journey.

Trap had moved straight up the east slope of the Sierra San Luis in Chihuahua, right along the continental divide, covering the 40 miles to the U.S. border in two days. As slyly as a marijuana smuggler, he slipped under the fence into the New Mexican panhandle in the dead of night. Little did he know, but that slink into the United States was the most important step of his life. He was no longer a thief in the night. He was now a royal member of an endangered species. No one could legally touch him.

When Trap reached the north end of the San Luis range, he turned west, following by instinct the old Cloverdale-Whitewater runway used by marauding Mexican wolves during the first half of the twentieth century when game became scarce south of the border. He crossed San Luis Pass and headed directly into a sheep corral, literally in the footsteps of his famous predecessor Old One Toe.

Old One Toe, who had left two other toes in a trap near Ruby, Arizona, went in and out of Mexico countless times in the early 1920s, frequently shopping that particular corral. He signed his work—dead lambs and calves with only a couple of bites ripped out of their flanks—

with a single scratch mark in the dust. He was finally killed by a government trapper who had been chasing him for four years.

Trap stole one sheep from the rancher at San Luis Pass, then kept discretely in the timber as he headed further north along the Animas Mountains, dropping down to the grasslands at Indian Creek.

"*B'doo, b'doo, b'doo.*"

This time it was the shrill of a killdeer that jostled Trap's eyes part way open as he lounged on his back for his second nap. The sky was the white blue of high noon. The creek was chortling close by. He shrugged his shoulders enjoying a small, grassy back scratch, cocked his head higher to feel the warm caress of the sun on the underside of his chin, and lollygagged back into a third snooze. He would stay awhile.

Trap spent all of November picking off livestock at ranches up and down the Animas Valley. For afternoon fun, he terrorized the local gopher holes, cramming his long unwelcome nose into the rodent-reeking parlors. He loved to pounce and destroy any fleeing residents, but he left the carcasses to rot, never cultivating a taste for rat. Besides, calves and lambs were plentiful, and although Indian Creek had once been a crossroad for wolves, the new generation of ranchers blamed all the kills on mountain lions. And before anyone got too outraged and organized an effort to find the predator, Trap's wanderlust got the better of him and he headed out on a ranch road that climbed over the Peloncillo Mountains into southeast Arizona.

He descended from the mountains by way of Skeleton Canyon where the outlaw Curly Bill Brocius and his gang once massacred a band of Mexican cattle thieves who were encroaching on Bill's rustling territory. The skeletons of the banditos, at least pieces of them, were still scattered in the canyon. Trap dropped into the San Bernardino Valley crossing the site where the Apache chief Geronimo surrendered in 1886. He passed south of the Chiricahua Mountains where another Apache chief Cochise hid his people during the last phase of the Indian Wars and the lone red Chiricahua Wolf prowled until 1916. The red wolf evaded trappers for years and even avoided wolf packs, preferring to stay alone haunting the camps of his Indian predecessors and striking the valley ranches precisely once every four days.

Trap moved through this territory at an even trot, undistracted by any ghosts from the past or any present livestock, until he dropped down into the broad, flat Sulphur Springs Valley, a high desert studded with windmills and water tanks and the purple haze of pecan groves. Grass was sparse and so were the houses. He spent his first night in an irrigated corn field.

At the crack of dawn, Trap was rattled awake by the cackling calls of hundreds and hundreds of sandhill cranes, V after V coming into the corn and landing all around him. Unfamiliar with the gangling birds, uncertain as to whether they were predator or prey, but not liking the looks of their long claws and sharp beaks, he did what came quick and natural. He dashed after two who had just landed, rolled himself up like a bowling ball and knocked them over before they had even gotten their wings tucked in. Two quick snaps and he had ripped off two chests for a tasty, corn-fed breakfast.

It was just that easy all winter. He came across an abandoned house that stood alone at the edge of a field, and he was just brazen enough to stay there, digging in under the back porch. It was a warm, dry nest during the rains which poured through more regularly than normal, the jet stream held far to the south this year by extreme Arctic cold. The old cottonwoods in the backyard, though leafless in winter, were filled on the sunny days with mourning doves tirelessly chanting their question, "*Who-who? Who-who?*" Trap explored all the nearby orchards and frequently found an apple on the ground, missed in the harvest. He cleaned his teeth on fallen pecans and pistachios.

Wandering one sunny afternoon to the north end of the valley, Trap discovered the playa, the dry bed of a prehistoric lake. The shallow, ten-mile-wide basin was partly filled with water in its northernmost section due to the rainy season. Approaching from the south over miles of dry sand, the water looked like a mirage, but it was real. It was the reason the sandhill cranes came to Sulphur Springs Valley for the winter, some from as far away as Siberia.

Thereafter, Trap visited the playa almost daily, taking rolling sand baths in the dry part of the lake bed or splashing and playing among the cranes who preferred wading in the water. He never attacked in the playa, and the cranes, secure in their numbers, accepted his presence with only a low level of suspicion. Dozing in the winter sunshine, Trap was as carefree as a Florida retiree. All he lacked was a piña colada and a Hawaiian shirt.

Chapter 21

THE HARDWARE

"We shall live again,
We shall live again."
Comanche Ghost Dance Song

It was noon when Mayor George P. Stone limped down the boardwalk of old downtown William, trying to appear nonchalant. He passed the black hole that used to be William Hardware, resolutely pushing aside any thought of the painful, life-changing crash he had made in the alleyway five years ago. Besides, he was more worried about what Dot would do to him if she caught him today. He pulled his Disneyland hat over his ears, looked both ways to see if there was anyone on the street who might recognize him, then he ducked into the Bucket of Beer Bar.

The full impact of the cigarette smoke and the aroma of stale alcohol, which he only had a hint of out on the street, set George off balance, and he reeled to the bar as if he'd already had one too many. The place was empty except for a few hard-drinking regulars hunched over their glasses at the bar. There was a heavyset man in a cowboy hat and a bird-like woman whose eyes darted to him immediately.

"Some meat and potatoes at last." She cackled. Her voice was raspy from heavy smoking and a breakfast of bourbon.

George headed to the opposite end of the bar and pulled up onto a stool beside the third patron. The man wore a red and black checkered wool hunting jacket with a big rip on the sleeve. He hadn't been hunting in decades. He leaned forward with his eyes closed, both big hands around a full glass of whiskey. One deep vertical line was set in each cheek accentuating the dead horse appearance of his long, narrow face. His hair was buzzed closely on the sides, but stood a full inch high, and straight up, on top. He had worn his hair that way for 30 years, ever since George had known him.

George ordered a Bud. A cowboy singer twanged at the juke box about a gambler who'd folded in the love department.

"How ya been, Howard?" George said after his beer came to him.

Startled, Howard Daugherty, owner of the burned-out William Hardware, opened his eyes and looked over at George. His blank brown stare gathered itself and he recognized the mayor.

"George. Guess I'm alive. How's your feet?"

"Guess I'm walking. How's the wife?"

"Ah, she's madder'n blazes at me."

"Yep. Mine's mad at me, too, and it's probably going to be worse tonight."

They both sipped for a little while.

"Downtown's sure gone to pot since the fire," George said.

"Yep."

"Shame to have that empty hole over there, next door."

"Yep."

"Could be earning you some money."

"Probly."

"Ever think of rebuilding the Hardware?"

"I think about it. Louise wants me to. She nags about it all the time, but I jes dunno. I come in here and nurse a whiskey. Don't really drink much. I think about rebuildin, but I can't visualize it. I just can't visualize it. You doin any buildin lately?"

"Haven't done anything commercial since the accident. Dot's against it. Last time I went out to buy a box of nails, I fell down a flight of stairs. She'd like me to push pencils from here on out, but I always have a few projects going. Hey, why don't you come take a ride with me. I have an idea that I've been wanting to talk to you about."

Howard, left his booze, got off his barstool and followed George out into the sunlight. It was the first time in a long spell he'd spent a noon out-of-doors. He squinted at the blue sky trying to remember what month it was.

"I sure don't need this jacket out here," and he peeled it off. It was March 1, seventy-two degrees.

George had gotten the seed of the idea while lying in his hospital bed five years ago when he was still floating with painkillers. Howard had been one of his first visitors after the surgery, thanking George for his heroic efforts to save the Hardware, but it wasn't that visit that George remembered clearly. It was the newspaper photo the next day, Howard Daugherty in a long slicker and high rubber boots sweeping black water out of his store, the burned face of his trophy moose hovering in the background. George looked into Howard's eyes in the photo, wondering if they might both be ruined men now.

George had searched the drab green walls of his hospital room for some color to fight the grayness that was closing in. He focused on a little pot of yellow chrysanthemums, whispering "Dot...Dot...Dot" as he faded into sleep. Even in his sleep he fought the yawning hole of fire, with his arms because his legs couldn't move, waving them above the sheets, stacking bricks. "Nothing contains fire like a brick wall," he murmured.

George drove past his own house, turned the corner and pulled into the back yard from the alley. There was no chance Dot would be home this time of day.

"Here's what I've been doing all winter," George said.

The two of them got out and walked over to the project: tier after tier of neatly stacked walls of cleaned bricks, the salvaged remains of the demolished Shell station.

"Nearly five thousand recycled red bricks."

"Ain't they kinda yella?" Howard asked.

"I got them out of an old yellow gas station. Why people think they have to go and paint a beautiful red brick, I can't figure out. Cheese, what a color. As I sat on the pile cleaning off the mortar, I was thinking I'd just build a double brick wall with the painted sides turned in. No one would ever know they'd been painted. But, you know, pretty soon the color stopped looking like yellow to me. It started looking more golden. I can envision a whole wall of gold."

Howard sat down on an overturned five-gallon paint bucket and studied the colored bricks.

"Nope, they're yella. Maybe you could build a wall with just a few of the yella sides out. It wouldn't be so loud."

George went on. "The trouble with the old Hardware was that it was built out of sticks. Bricks are better. Bricks don't burn. The Big Bad Wolf himself couldn't blow down a Hardware built out of bricks. Why don't we take these bricks and rebuild your store?"

Howard was silent for a while. Finally, he stood up from the bucket.

"George, like I said, I've been doin a lota thinkin and I jes can't see me sellin hardware anymore. But you know, Louise is still young and she loved workin at the store with the china and crystal. She was in charge of all that and she's miserable without it. We still have quite a bit of her inventory that was stashed in the basement. The fire didn't touch it. How about if we build a brick store for Louise and her dishes? Not many of them yella ones turned to the outside."

George put out his hand and Howard grabbed it.

George dropped Howard off back at the Town Square, and he glanced over into Armory Park as he drove past. At Virginia's request, he had authorized the Town Parks Department to turn the sprinklers back on and, even this early in spring, the grass was a brilliant green. He noticed there were flowers blooming as well. Scattered throughout the park like small bouquets were orange, yellow and white African daisies. Hadn't Virginia done some kind of flower experiment here? He quickly pulled into a parking spot and had a good cry. Virginia had moved away and was living in Tucson, Cynthia was expecting a baby any day now, he and Howard were recycled men.

Afterwards, George stopped at the drug store for a bottle of Scope, gargled in the truck, and spat in the parking lot. He did that a few more times during the afternoon, and he bobbed in the kitchen door at 5:30 with a big smile, maybe a little too big. Dot, stirring at the stove, was suspicious immediately. He could tell by the slight movement of her nose that even all afternoon in the sunshine didn't completely remove the Bucket of Beer from his clothing.

"What are you going to build now?" Her lips were in a straight line, but she turned back to the soup and gave it a big smile.

FROM THE JOURNAL OF HENRY DAVID TARANTULA

THUNDERBIRD

It is said that thunder and lightning are produced by a great bird, the thunderbird. His shadow is the thundercloud; the sound of thunder comes from his flapping wings. His eyes, his flashing eyes, send forth lightning, the zigzag lines originating in his heart. In my dream, the thunderbird came to me. When he saw me he said, "You are the offspring of a raven." In my dream, I am fed by ravens.

Chapter 22

MARGARITA'S GHOST

"Dreams are but incoherent combinations of waking ideas, and there is a hint of recollection even in the wildest visions of sleep."
James Mooney, *The Ghost-Dance Religion and the Sioux Outbreak of 1890*

Even in the sunny Sulphur Springs Valley, the cold settled in at night, the dew collected on the sparse grass, and Trap dreamed. With his three good legs, he ran in midair and he woke up exhausted. The ghost of his right back leg returned and throbbed. It was a restlessness he shared with the cranes, who gathered in large groups by day, their noisy banter seeming more serious. Instead of flying in random groups of six to twelve, they clung together in Vs of thirty or more, circling the valley. Trap would lay half-buried in the sand of the playa, watching, sensing their new energy. In early March, the cranes began heading out in drove by clamorous drove, their formations like arrows pointing straight north.

It didn't bother Trap to see his steady diet migrating away. The meat was rich and exotic, but he was constantly pestered by the feathers that stuck in his teeth and clung to his chin and fur no matter how much he rolled in the sand. He wasn't interested in following the flock. He was listening to a calling of his own. When he circled each night before sleep, he more often than not lay down facing west, a range rarely entered by wolves, though Margarita had traveled there.

Margarita was a white queen of a wolf. From 1916 to 1924 she made a circuit through Arizona, covering Cochise, Pima and even Maricopa Counties. She traveled with a retinue of up to sixty coyotes, who never dared approach her, but hung in the background waiting for her next killing binge. Sometimes Margarita would take thirty sheep in one night, sometimes fifty.

The ranchers posted her name across the countryside like any outlaw's, a $500 reward on her head. They called her a murderer, a fiend and a monster. Some believed she was possessed by the devil himself. They would never have believed she only killed for the song. After a night's plunder, Margarita would retreat to a high outpost, sit on her tail, close her eyes and seem to smile. She waited for the coyotes to slip in from all directions and have their feast. Then, without fail, one of them would let out a loud laugh. The other coyotes would immediately take up the chorus. One musical wave after another would rise from the killing field, sometimes intricate harmony, other times utter babel like a tree full of starlings. When the passion subsided into yips, Margarita would lick her lips and disappear.

In the end, of course, the bounty hunters got her. They strung up her body by the heels from a mesquite tree and they all had their pictures taken.

Mid-March, when the last of the cranes were on their merry way north, Trap headed west, following the phantom of the white wolf Margarita. He got on a dirt road and trotted for two days and nights. The soft surface was easy on his feet, and he stopped only long enough to hide from the occasional pickup truck, to mark his scent on large landmarks, and to defecate on strewn beer cans. The road led him up over the Dragoon Mountains, through a tight forest of oaks that he didn't bother to hunt. When Trap emerged from the trees one early morning, the land fell away into the cactus and creosote of the Lower Sonoran Desert. The rainy winter had wrought heavy dividends, and Trap gazed upon fields and fields of yellow-orange poppies. Despite his keen senses, he was not attuned to the flashy color. What brought him to his knees was the wave of intense perfume and heady pollen. He slept all day in the flowers.

FROM THE JOURNAL OF HENRY DAVID TARANTULA

I saw her. She is a ghost. Emerging out of the field of watermelons. Running down the hill like white vapor. She can't be real. She is a dream. Midnight flashing from her eyes. Lightning zigzagging from her heart. She has electrified me. The water hits me, knocks me down, and I am carried away by the river. What did she see in the Window? Something clear? Something blue? Is that all? Is that enough? Did she see the magic rabbit?

Chapter 23

THE RIVER

"We have an unknown distance yet to run; an unknown river yet to explore. What falls there are, we know not."
John Wesley Powell, *The Exploration of the Colorado River and its Canyons*

Bruce "The Snake" Smith seemed less of a snake now and more of an engineer. He was at least somebody I knew on the University campus of 40,000 students, and he had a vehicle. That came in handy on rare occasions, but I mostly avoided him. It was hard to take the chat about his frat brothers and his vast knowledge of electrical circuitry. Mom thought he "sounded nice."

The biology building was four stories tall, and the front door opened into a glassed-in stairway that ran up all four levels and doubled as a vertical tropical terrarium. Dieffenbachias and Ficus trees planted at the ground floor had grown as high as the second story. It was rumored that they were fed blood by the microbiology students.

The modern classrooms, auditoriums really, held hundreds of students at a time, and the closest undergraduates came to a professor was viewing a small head above a podium down front, with a large voice reaching us in the higher tiers by microphone. My laboratories were held in the old chemistry building, which had high ceilings with hanging, buzzing fluorescent lights, warped, peeling floors, old wooden drawers that wouldn't open or close easily and were filled with incomplete supplies, and a tinge of hydrogen sulfide gas in the air.

I loved it. No one knew I was the daughter of a mayor. I wore stretched out turtlenecks and ragged sweatpants under Henry David's long Navy pea coat. He'd left a handful of wool lint in one of the pockets and I held it as I walked between classes. It rained and rained all winter making up for the scorching summer. The low ceiling of clouds and clinging humidity gave me a secure, enclosed feeling in spite of the big city where I was now living.

Between storms I'd sit on a dry curb reading a book and no one thought I was bookish. Others were doing the same. There was always a chance that Henry David might walk by. I didn't know where he had gone after he moved out of the cave. He just disappeared. It was possible he had decided to enroll here, or more likely he was at Arizona State University in Phoenix since that's where his parents lived. Maybe he had set off on a long journey or had just taken an ordinary job. On clear days I rode my bike off campus and into the neighborhoods. There were huge white houses with red mission tile roofs and the population per capita of mourning doves was Malthusian.

"*Who-who? Who-who?*"

Quail ran around under trees in the front yards.

"*Cha-tah'-qua. Cha-tah'-qua.*"

Rain or shine, every Friday night there were street dances on the campus mall. The bands—never Henry David's—were protected under a large canvas tent, while the students were left out in the weather. I usually danced alone, insatiably, hiding inside the enormous pea coat and a dark curtain of hair.

The dormitories were atrocious. Four of us were crammed into a room the size of my bedroom at home. There were two bunk beds and four three-foot long desks, and it always smelled like marijuana. The pea coat took up three-quarters of my closet space and my roommates insisted that I have it cleaned before I hung it up. No one appreciated my Farmer John hours either, nor acted considerately when I went to bed with earplugs. I could only hang out on the lawn or hide out in the library for so long before I had to go face the claustrophobic living space.

"Tomorrow I'd better wear my big white cotton underwear," my roommate Darla drawled during a typical late-night conversation. She was from Mississippi and slept in the bunk below me. She was talking to Susan Jane and Tiffaney who were sitting in the bottom bunk across the two-foot corridor between beds. Sometimes I think they forgot I was hovering in the upper bunk. I didn't think Darla even had any big cotton underwear. She shopped for lingerie religiously, adding something silky, brightly colored and tiny to her top drawer at least weekly. Her most sedate underwear I had witnessed had leopard spots on it. "It's the only way I will ever be able to say no to him."

"Darla, if you wear big cotton underwear, it's going to make a very bad first impression. He's going to think you're unimaginative in bed," Susan Jane said. She was painting her toenails purple.

"But the point is, if I'm wearing whities, he'll never see them because I'd be too embarrassed. If I wear a thong on the first date, he'll think I'm crazy in bed," Darla said.

"Ben is so gorgeous." Tiffaney was giggling. She had a green mudpack on her face. "Why don't you compromise and wear some lacy panties."

Susan Jane had some input on that. "I've heard that lacy panties make men think you'll start out saying yes then change your mind at the last minute."

I lowered my head over the edge and appeared upside down to Darla in the lower bunk, my hair almost touching the floor.

"What does it mean if a *guy* wears *no* underwear?" I said to her.

Darla shrieked. Maybe it was the hair.

"Oh my God, Virginia," Susan Jane said. "You are such a slut." That produced a chorus of giggles.

I much preferred, in fact longed to hear, the midnight sound of Cynthia in the bathroom throwing up.

In March, the quail began hatching their broods, and the Tucson front yards were parade grounds for lines of their little chicks. Flower beds were bursting with velvety petunias and taunting me with apricot, butterscotch, and cream-colored daisies. I finally gave in and accepted a date with Bruce Smith. We were going to go inner tubing on the Gila River.

On a Saturday morning Bruce picked me up in his truck and we drove for about an hour to Sheep's Crossing. We would put in there and float seven miles to a sandy beach called Hooligan's Bar. He said there would be a big frat party going on at Hooligan's—nothing fancy, just a sand bar and beer—and we could hitch a ride back up to the truck. For the rest of the drive, Bruce theorized that human behavior could be explained and thus predicted by solving, via a computer program, a series of thousands of simultaneous equations representing biological, psychological and social variables. He was wearing shorts and his legs were pretty hairy but underdeveloped.

"What if you're crazy?" I asked him. "How can you predict behavior then?"

"Your hair is so beautiful," he replied. It was in a single braid which I had wound up tightly in a knot on the back of my head with a wooden skewer holding it in place. "Why don't you wear it down?"

"Do you ever play in the Dirt band anymore?"

"We broke up after the election party, though Mustache Mike is playing with the Regressions. It's a hot band up in Phoenix right now. Maybe the two of us could go up to Phoenix sometime and take in some music?"

I treated it like a rhetorical question and didn't answer. He didn't say anything about Henry David.

There were two theories about tubing the Gila: You either tie yourself to your tube or you don't. Bruce, being a serious engineer, tied himself to me, me to Tube Number One, Tube Number One to Tube Number Two, and Tube Number Two to a big plastic bag containing lunch, drinking water, and towels. He really didn't want to lose those tubes, which he borrowed from the frat house. We stripped down to our swim suits, though Bruce kept his T-shirt on, and crammed our clothes into the plastic bag as well. Then we slithered down the embankment at Sheep's Crossing.

The Gila was in full flood, muddy brown and roaring like a superhighway. As we got close to it, the uneven motion of currents and eddies and the unrelenting noise made me dizzy and short of breath. For a moment I couldn't tell if the water was rushing away or I was reeling backwards. Dozens of swallows were soaring about a foot off the water lunching on insects, their quick turns and haphazard patterns adding to the confusion.

"B'doo, b'doo, b'doo." A bird I couldn't see was shrieking at us.

I might have chickened out, but Bruce tossed the plastic bag in Tube Number Two, flopped himself into Tube Number One, grabbed me by my bright pink bikini, and pulled me in on top of him. We were quickly aboard a mighty movement across the face of Arizona. The shining snowfields of the Pinaleño Mountains, dissolved by the spring sun, plummeted toward the inescapable magnetism of the Gulf of California, dragging with them the reddish dirt of the hillsides and the dark soil of the grasslands trampled loose by cattle. I was kicking like a pink flamingo.

The river soon widened a bit, and the pace became more sluggish as we plowed through some flat farmlands. It was a little uncomfortable, two in a tube, but when Bruce would stop talking for a minute, I started to enjoy the gentle lap of the water. We meandered under an arbor of cottonwoods, which had not yet leafed out. They stood like gray vertical brushstrokes along the river, their tops a labyrinth of silvery webs.

"This hair clip is dangerous. Mind if I take it off?" he asked as he pulled out my skewer. The bun was released, but my braid was intact and wound down into the water. Thank goodness a bloated beaver floated by belly up. Bruce had to paddle with both hands to get us away from it.

"Have you ever tubed this river before?" I asked.

"No, but I got some instructions from my brothers at the House." He was playing with my hair again. "They said stay away from downed trees and drink lots of beer."

"Why are we doing it during flood season?"

"Makes it more exciting. Are you nervous?" Now he was touching my leg.

"So, do you ever hear anything from Henry David Tarantula?" I imagined Henry David wandering in the desert, yelling at the big black birds, following his nose like a willow stick to water.

"You didn't hear? Old Hen croaked off this past winter. You know his parents moved here from Pennsylvania for his health. He never should have been living in a cave out in the desert with all his allergies. He caught pneumonia, and then with the asthma..."

There was a roaring in my ears. I thought it was my own blood, but it was the Gila River crashing into a huge, downed cottonwood in our path. Bruce began frantically paddling to try to get us to the other side of the river and around the tree. The only effect he had was to drive our inner tube in a circle and splash a lot of water in my face. Our tube went right into the tree and flipped.

I was slammed against the tree and the bottom of the river by the wild, muddy water. There was no up or down. Everything was in a fast, close circle. I was powerless against the current.

When I left home and Daddy was packing my bags and bike into the truck for our trip to Tucson, Mom cornered me in the kitchen.

"It was you, wasn't it?"

"What are you talking about?"

"You know what I'm talking about. I recognized your painting on those watermelons. You really hurt your father." She crammed a thick wad of twenty-dollar bills in my pocket, but she didn't kiss me good-bye.

I regretted that my parents would have to identify my body bloated like a beaver, but otherwise I rode easily, almost happily in the current, waiting for my lungs to fill with water.

To my surprise, Bruce dragged me up. At least as far up as he could considering the ropes and tubes were hopelessly tangled around the downed tree and me. I got one hand on a branch above water and one toe of my tennis shoe jammed into the unstable gravel of the bottom. A rope burned at my waist to get me back down, and another had me by the throat.

My head bobbed in and out of the water as the current rattled by, but when I could catch a breath, I yelled, "Watermelons suck."

It was my swim suit top that had me by the neck, and Bruce was able to get that off quickly. That was a huge relief and got my head further out of the water. He kept diving to free the rope around my waist. With my free hand I took off my silver-lensed sunglasses with the pink and blue bubbles. I laid them down on the Gila and watched them float away. In the water near the bank I saw the reflection of a bush covered with bright orange flowers, but I couldn't see any such colorful bush on shore. Even after Bruce got me out and I crawled around in the sand topless, I couldn't find those orange flowers.

Bruce managed to save both tubes, too, but all that was left of the bag of food and clothing was a small piece of black plastic. He gave me his wet T-shirt.

I curled up into a hard ball, my arms clasped around my shins, my face pressed into my knees, and I was shivering hard. Bruce tried to snuggle up, but I shrugged him away.

"Leave me alone."

He retreated a few feet and sat on a tube. The sun and the sand felt like warm hands on my back. The shirt began to dry out and flutter in the breeze, and tears started flowing down my legs.

Bruce tried again. He didn't say a word, but gently unleashed my hair and spread it across my back to dry. That was good until he started to talk.

"Come on. Cheer up. How about if we get back on the river and try it again? It's only five more miles to the beer."

"I don't want to go."

He kept talking. "I've heard that in China, if a man saves a woman's life, she becomes his slave. Come to think of it, I've saved you from disaster twice." He put his hands on my arms, drew me backwards and nuzzled my shoulder.

That was it. I sprang upright, probably bruising myself on his front teeth, grabbed an innertube and hung it around myself as a makeshift bathrobe, and started walking upstream.

"I'm going back to the truck."

He followed dejectedly at a distance.

Chapter 24

BAPTISM

"Till the gossamer thread you fling catch somewhere, o my soul."
Walt Whitman, *"A Noiseless Patient Spider"*

Cynthia was going through a battle with a raging, flooding river at the same time I was. When I got back to the dorm, there was an urgent message to call home. Brick Palmer Stolz, seven pounds two ounces, was born at 1:20 p.m. on March 21, the first day of spring.

"It's a boy, it's a boy, it's a boy." I ran down the hallway knocking on doors and hugging people I had never even said hi to before. The deep black hole that Bruce had gouged in me with his news about Henry David created a shocking capacity for joy. Spring break started in a week, and Daddy was coming to pick me up and take me home.

Home was like walking into a department store during the Christmas rush, everyone stressed and happy. Cynthia's face was all broken out, which was high on her list of complaints, and the baby did get jaundice. Mom was taking meals over every day even though she had already filled Cynthia's freezer. Everett looked like he'd been sleepless since Cynthia went into labor, which was probably close to the truth, and he couldn't walk across a room without stumbling on something. Daddy somehow got his picture on the front page with his new grandson.

Brick was like a tiny blond monkey and he loved to stretch his face and hands. When he squalled, we all ran to help, but Cynthia, proudly, was the only one who could console him. Nobody called him Brick yet; everyone called him Pooh.

To make things even more hectic, Cynthia decided that the baby should be baptized while I was home on break, and she asked me to be godmother. Mom started shopping for a Christening gown and I was put in charge of a brunch. Daddy kept out from underfoot in his shop, working on a gift.

I thought I would get to hold the baby during the ceremony, but Cynthia did.

"What do you ask of God's Church for Brick Palmer?" Father O'Ryan began. I stood next to Everett's brother Robert, the godfather, and it reminded me of Cynthia's wedding three years ago. We'd been teamed up then, too. He was older than Everett and twice as wide. Same priest, too, and he asked us both, "Are you ready to help the parents of this child in their duty as Christian parents?"

"We are." We had rehearsed that. We were supposed to answer "I do" to the rest of the questions.

"Do you reject Satan?" Satan is a skinny, spindly creature shaped more or less like a man but with a tail and purple. He has highly-placed, pointy ears, tiny horns, a single nostril, and a mustache like a cat. Everyone else said, "I do."

"And all his works?"

"I do." All but me.

"And all his empty promises?"

Robert nudged me as if I were ruining the Baptism.

"Do you believe in God..." the Father droned on asking us more questions to which I didn't have an answer. Cynthia and Daddy were big churchgoers. They probably would have turned charismatic if Mom didn't pour ice water on them once in a while. I was more in Mom's camp. I thought about running my hands around the rough, cool rock of the Window, feeling unworthy, finally daring to look through the opening. All I saw was an empty sky.

Father O'Ryan sprinkled on the holy water and Pooh let out a scream that made me proud to be his godmother. Cynthia couldn't get him to stop so Father sped through the rest of the ceremony.

"Holy Mary, Mother of God..."

"Pray for us."

"Saint John the Baptist..."

"Pray for us."

"Saint Joseph..."

"Pray for us."

"Saints Peter and Paul..."

"Pray for us."

"Saints Bartholomew and Polycarp..." I guess Father O'Ryan had really struggled to find patron saints to match the name Brick Palmer, or else he was making a slightly acidic hint to the parents that they should have chosen names more traditionally Catholic.

"Pray for us," they said.

"St. Paul will be fine for his patron saint." I finally made my response.

"Amen," everyone said.

As an offering of penance to my father, I served watermelon at the brunch. It was scooped into tiny balls and put back into the scraped rind along with cantaloupe, honeydew and strawberries. Even Cynthia raved about how beautiful it looked. I had baked for two days—cherry scones, blueberry muffins and banana bread from the box, and Pillsbury cinnamon rolls from the can. Homemade pecan rolls were way beyond me. While I set out the pastries, coffee and orange juice on Cynthia's dining room table, Mom warmed up a tray of sausages and whipped up a huge skillet of scrambled eggs.

Pooh had worn himself out being baptized, and Cynthia had tucked him into the crib. Everett was practically drooling he wanted so badly to crawl into bed, too. Daddy, however, was wide awake and ebullient. Cynthia had to keep shushing him so he wouldn't wake the baby.

"I can't wait any longer," Daddy said about halfway through breakfast.

"I want to show you what I have for Cynthia and the baby. Everett and I moved it into the den at six o'clock this morning."

Both families traipsed down Cynthia's hallway carrying our plates, tiptoeing past the nursery, and entering a small room at the back of the house that was called the den. The huge gift was sitting under a white sheet, which Daddy whipped off with a flourish.

The guests were all a bit stunned. Polished, showy grained, mahogany, almost red, dwarfing the room, shining white keys, it was an upright piano.

"The baby won't be playing that for a while, George," Everett's father said with a deep ho-ho.

"You have to think ahead on these things, Ralph. A family needs a piano. Where else do you put the baby photos and graduation and wedding photos?"

We didn't have a piano ourselves.

"Everett and I pulled this instrument out of a cave. I thought it was a piece of junk but the piano tuner told me a cave was the best place in the world to put a piano. The cool, even temperature is good for the sound board. This sound board is in perfect shape."

He opened the front revealing the strings.

"This is all it was when I got it. A bunch of naked strings. It wouldn't even play one note. Come to find out, there was a huge black notebook full of papers wedged down inside it. Once I got that out, it made plenty of noise, but I had to put on all new ivories."

"Oh, I love it," Cynthia said. She caressed the mahogany and sat down on the little claw-legged stool in front of it.

"I'd better not play it now. I'll wake the baby."

Cynthia didn't even know how to play middle C.

"Daddy, that's *my* piano," I piped up.

"What do you need a piano for, Virginia? You don't even live in town anymore. I'm the one who pulled it out of the cave, and Cynthia has a family now."

"Where did you put the papers you found in it?"

"They were just full of chicken scratches. You couldn't even read it. I gave them to your mother."

I found Mom in the blurring circle of faces. She stepped forward and took my shaking plate.

"Bottom drawer of your dresser," she said.

It was only three-quarters of a mile to our house, and I did it all at a dead run. Mom must have left the party soon after me. I was on my knees in front of the dresser, still gasping for air, Henry David's black book clutched to me like it was my own baby, when I heard her pull into the carport.

"He's dead. He's dead," I screamed at her when she came into my room. "Why didn't you tell me?"

"Henry David Tarantula? Henry David Tarantula is dead? I didn't know. I never saw anything in the paper. I always read the obituaries."

"Henry David Tarantula is not his real name." It was like the river hit me again and held me down under the cottonwood. Mom hugged me as hard as I was hugging the black notebook and I kept slamming my head into her chest.

FROM THE JOURNAL OF HENRY DAVID TARANTULA

SCIENCE PROJECT

It's the stupidest science project I ever heard of. It can't be real. She's just another giggling college chick chasing after me. She's thumbing her nose at my platform. I say stamp out science! Techno-farmers are tearing up the landscape with tractors, draining the water table, polluting the river with phosphates and sulfides. She proves my point about the absurdity of science, wearing lace into the desert that's bound to catch on every passing thorn, positing an experiment involving perky orange daisies. Her fussy presence invades my morning solitude. Her hair is never out of that tight knot. Her bright flowers wave below me like little bits of laughter. What is there to laugh about? Rain hisses when it hits my shoulders. I am a hostile environment for any seed.

Chapter 25

VIRGINIA AND THE WOLF

"Under his arm he carried an old music-book to press plants; in his pocket, his diary and pencil, a spy-glass for birds, microscope, jack-knife, and twine."
Ralph Waldo Emerson, *"Thoreau," The Atlantic, 1862*

It was springtime in the desert. The bellies of lizards turned turquoise blue. Exuberant tarantulas with gleaming eyes stretched their hairy legs in meter-long leaps, and the grasshoppers sang. A cactus wren couple dove into the thorns of a cholla to make a nest. A usually arrogant male cardinal, redder than ever, offered his dull wife a few seeds. Jackrabbits delivered their babies under creosote bushes. Four sparrow hawks roosted one on top of the other on an old saguaro while a tiny elf owl hid in his nest inside. The winter storms had predestined a flashy carpet of yellow brittlebush, orange poppies, purple larkspur, red ocotillos and even a few African daisies. Martha Benson would have been pleased.

I left the house early to drive out to the old Benson place. Mom had stuck a peanut butter sandwich and a thermos of coffee in my hand on my way out the door, and I threw them in my backpack with the science kit. The science kit was kind of silly. It had come with a field notebook, a magnifying glass, a bird book, pocketknife, and a few other odds and ends that were sure to please a ten-year-old, which is when I got it for Christmas. I replaced the bird book with a good Peterson's Guide, the pocketknife with a Swiss army knife, and have been through a great pile of little field notebooks. It was just habit that I brought it today.

I was possessed by such lethargy after the emotion of yesterday's Baptism. I had driven up an hour ago and still hadn't gotten out of the blue International. I finally remembered the coffee and poured myself a cup in the thermos lid. Mom had put in plenty of cream and sugar. The warmth of the cup in my hands and the steam in my face as I breathed into it made me sleepy, but the caffeine kicked in by the time I finished the cup. I rolled down the window, laid my head in the opening, and looked up at the clouds. From horizon to horizon, the sky was filled with small fair weather puffs. The backdrop was baby blue and the clouds themselves were brilliant white.

Henry David's black notebook contained more than a hundred pages, each one scrawled backwards from the righthand edge to the left, no margins, and decorated with arrows that intertwined the letters, making it even more indecipherable. I had finally put it back into my bottom dresser drawer last night. I wouldn't try to read it yet. I would take it back to the university, spread it out on a well-lit library table, and transcribe it.

The moisture in the air carried the fragrance of the reborn, flowering desert, and I could hear that Cholla Creek was running. I emerged stiffly from the cocoon of the truck. I circled the old house and wandered back to the ruins of "Squeaky" the windmill that lay lifelessly on its side. It was early enough in the spring that the new growth hadn't completely overtaken the fallen relic, and I could survey it clearly in the grass. Surprisingly, the metal blades were still intact, though rusty. It was the wooden trellis that had given out and lay in pieces like old bones.

Further back toward Cholla Canyon, my experimental plot from the previous fall had sprouted a few daisies but was mostly filled with a batch of opportunistic, noxious weeds facilitated by my disturbance of the soil. I had created more harm than beauty. From here, the noise of the creek was irresistible.

It was a completely different scene from what I had hiked through in September. The creek was full and bubbling, and the banks were green with Resurrection bush and moss. There was a wide, flat muddy beach where I could clearly read who had come for a drink that morning. There were the messy scrawls of birds mixed with the dainty prints of squirrels and, lying down and looking closely, I detected the tiny traces of a mouse. I found the hoof prints of a deer and the deep rut of a cow. I hadn't realized anyone was still ranching in this area. Then I saw something that sent me sprinting for the truck. Daddy always had a few cans of nails and screws rolling around in the back.

I dumped the coffee can of nails into the bed of the International and took the can, found a long screwdriver in the truck's built-in toolbox, grabbed the cup from my thermos, loaded it all into my pack and chugged back to the creek. I was really going to get some use out of the science kit.

For all these years I had been lugging around a small but heavy bag of plaster of Paris that came in the kit. Many times I had thought of throwing it out with the child's bird book and pocketknife, but adolescent hope had kept it in there. At the bank of the creek a little distance downstream from the tracked area, I emptied the contents of the bag into the coffee can and added two thermos cups of water from the creek, stirring with the screwdriver. When it seemed like the perfect consistency, I headed back to the mud, fearing I might have been hallucinating. No, there it was again, and I poured the plaster of Paris into the track.

I looked at my watch to time the full twelve minutes prescribed in the directions on the bag. Crawling around on my hands and knees, carefully making a second inspection of the surrounding area, I saw two other light disturbances, but at only one point had the animal sunk perceptibly into mud. Suddenly I became aware of an unusual quietness in the air. It seemed as if the birds and even the insects had hushed. I stood up quickly and scanned the desert. No movement, no eyes, no sudden color, yet a haunting, watchful presence.

At twelve minutes I got out my Swiss army knife and cut around the plaster cast, working the blade well under the mold. It easily lifted out. I went down to the creek again, dipped the mold into the water, and scrubbed away all the mud. As I brought it out clean, it seemed even more real in the plaster than on the ground. The hair on the back of my neck began to tickle. I had captured every claw, every pad. It was bigger than any coyote's print or any dog's. It was bigger than my own hand.

I emptied my lunch bag and carefully packed the plaster cast inside. I loaded my equipment into the backpack, unwrapped my peanut butter sandwich and left it on a rock.

"Don't worry, I'll keep your secret," I said to the desert as I headed for the truck. "And I'll bring you another present."

FROM THE JOURNAL OF HENRY DAVID TARANTULA

It is September. Is that the beginning or the end of the year? It is the beginning and the end. I have swept the bats from the belfry of the cave and deposited my belongings, but before I begin my residency, I will walk to the Window. I seek a vision. I follow in the footsteps of the Apache dreamers who came before me, may their spirits be with me.

The Window is located near the top of the San Miguel Mountains about 50 miles, as the tarantula crawls, from my Santa Isabella cave. I will take the high road to avoid the heat and find water. From here, I will hike up Rose Canyon and traverse the Santa Isabellas at an elevation of about 6,000 feet. I will cross Bloomington Pass that connects the Isabellas with the San Miguels and walk up and down San Miguel peaks to the westernmost end, then down Cholla Canyon to the Window. I will come home to the cave via the low road, hoping the weather has cooled, dipping into town at night to fill my water bottles from some unsupervised garden hose.

And so I begin my life in the desert with a journey. In my pack I have a fiberfill sleeping bag, a small tarp, camp stove and a bottle of white gas, matches, topo maps, flashlight, two plastic bottles for water, a cookpot and a spoon, bar of soap, a baggie of marijuana and pipe, two rolls of toilet paper, a harmonica, and an inhaler. I wear a sound pair of army boots, my only spare clothing is a watch cap, my only food is six pounds of raisins. For weaponry, I have my notebook and two stubby pencils plus a knife to keep the pencils sharp and, when a really important thought comes to me, I can hack it onto a tree.

Chapter 26

RAINBOW

"What sort of science is that which enriches the understanding but robs the imagination?"
Henry David Thoreau, *Journal, 1851*

"Daddy, I want to do another science project." I had poked my head into his workshop.

Daddy swung around with a guilty look on his face, arms widespread, possibly to hide what he had on the workbench. "Sure, Virginia, anything. Come on in. I'm just doing a little recycling here. Someone gave me an old, uh, TV. Let me give you a tour of my buckets."

He didn't think I could tell a TV from an air conditioner? It looked to me like he was finally getting around to recycling the air conditioner Henry David had smashed up at the press conference. Mom must have told him everything.

"I've got clear glass, brown glass, green glass, paper, cardboard, tin cans, aluminum cans, pot metal, number one copper, number two copper, light iron, cast iron, yellow brass and stainless steel." He rattled off the list pointing at each bucket in a line that surrounded the workbench.

"How much metal can you recycle out of an air conditioner?"

He moved over to the anvil and with a hand sledge started smashing aluminum cans from the family repository box that he had brought out from the den. He had a well-polished technique for getting the can to the anvil to the hammer to the bucket, both arms moving in opposite circles.

I meandered over to the north wall and noticed he had eleven and a half horseshoes nailed around the doorway.

"Your friend was right about air conditioners. Worthless rattletraps. You can't get enough metal out of an air conditioner to pay for the gas to get the rest to the dump. And the air they spew out is about as pleasant as the atmosphere of a cave. Oops." He sped on. "I sure plan to stick with the old Arizona swamp cooler. Now there was a simple, practical invention."

I think it was as close as he could come to a condolence.

"What's this hole?" My foot had just plunged into a small gap in the otherwise cement floor.

"That's Gray Squirrel's hole." He stopped pounding the cans and really cheered up. "He's been living in here on and off for a couple of years. He steals pecans from the trees down the block at Shorty's house and hides them behind the wood pile over there. He had a tunnel under the door, and you should have heard the fuss he kicked up the day I decided to pour a cement slab out here. To shut him up, I finally laid a concrete block over his hole to preserve the entry way, and I poured the cement around that.

I went over to the wood pile to look for the stash of nuts.

"Do you remember the old windmill at the Benson place?"

"Of course. That thing keeled over shortly after Martha did. Oops."

"Do you think you could get that windmill standing back up again and pumping water? I was out there this morning and it looks like the blades are okay. It's just the trestle that's broken. I'm interested in desert ecology, specifically the impact of a water hole on a heretofore dry area. For example, will animals relocate there? How will they interact with each other? Will they establish some sort of drinking order? Etcetera, etcetera."

"Old Martha would love that."

"Would the project have to be approved by the County since the County now owns the land?"

As Town mayor he loved pulling one over on the County. "The County will undoubtedly say no for liability reasons. We won't bother to ask."

"How do you raise a windmill?"

"I'm sure the Waldon can manage it. I'll drive out there this week and look it over. I suppose you want this done before you leave for school on Sunday?"

I wanted it so bad. He could see it in my face.

"Okay, you want this done before you leave for school on Sunday."

At six o'clock on Saturday morning, Daddy put the Waldon on the trailer, hitched it up to the International and called Everett.

"You weren't asleep, were you?"

"Yes. And I've been up three times so far with the baby." Cynthia never let him sleep either. He was on baby duty at night.

"Well, now that you're up, how about taking a little ride with me? Only take an hour."

"Okay, okay," he said, upon the fifth urgent kick from Cynthia.

"This is going to be an interesting project," Daddy called out the truck window to Everett as my bleary-eyed brother-in-law staggered out his front door. "You won't need that stuff." He was referring to Everett's hard hat and lunch bag.

"Oh yeah? I know your 'hour' and 'interesting projects.'" His hard hat, rarely used at his job in the chemistry lab at the copper mine, always went home with him on weekends. When he saw me in the truck, he was livid.

"If this is one of your stupid science projects, I'm going back to bed."

"Oh, get in," Daddy said. "I'm telling you, this is going to be interesting."

Everett squeezed into the truck with us, slammed his hard hat on, leaned against the window and fell asleep, completely undisturbed by the rattling the hat made on the glass with every imperfection of the road.

Daddy's plan for raising a windmill was every bit as bizarre as Don Quixote's attempt to joust one, and Everett's assigned task hardly appealed to the tired man's imagination.

"Dig me four holes ten inches deep right where I've marked the ground. Make them big enough to drop in a concrete block."

"Can't we do that with the Waldon?"

"Naw, I don't want to mess up the whole yard just to get four little holes, and I don't want to take the chance of injuring that water pipe sticking up there in the middle," he said as he dragged lumber off the truck.

Everett dug, Daddy rebuilt the trestle upon which the windmill gear box and blades were mounted, I pulled noxious weeds out of my old experimental plot, and a black cloud rolled in from the southwest.

"Just where I always wanted to be in a thunderstorm." Everett was shouting in my direction. "Standing next to a windmill tower."

Daddy verified that the windmill mechanism still seemed in good shape. The rotors needed some WD-40, which he sprayed on liberally. The central water pipe coming out of the ground was badly rusted and had snapped off when the whole thing came down. Daddy said he would have the pipe welded back together later. Until then we wouldn't know for sure if the differential behind the rotors had frozen up with rust or if the thing could still pump water. For now we were going to raise the structure on its new legs and drop it into Everett's four holes. It weighed two thousand pounds. We really needed a crane.

Daddy fired up the Waldon and drove it off the trailer. He detached the utility bucket and backed away from it. He was going to use the blades that supported the bucket as a forklift. The deep-throated diesel, spewing black smoke, tenderly loosened the prostrate windmill, which was partly buried in a tangle of weeds and dirt, with the finesse of a pastry chef working out the first wedge of pie.

"Cheese 'n crackers gul durn son of a bee." Daddy was as noisy as the tractor as he coaxed the wooden trestle right up to the edge of Everett's holes, now lined with cement blocks to provide a solid housing for the legs of the windmill. We were ready to tilt the windmill upright, and the cloud was getting closer.

Daddy unhitched the trailer from the truck and had Everett drive it around to the foot end of the windmill. Everett lined the truck up perfectly with the direction of the trestle on the ground and about 20 feet away. Daddy pulled cable out of the winch on the front of the International and attached it to a crossbar high up on the windmill trestle.

"First I'll lift her as high as I can with the Waldon," Daddy said, "Then when I give you the signal, you start winching her up."

"Are you sure this is safe?" Daddy didn't answer, just waved the question off with an impatient hand.

It looked beautiful on paper. Daddy positioned the Waldon at the top end of the windmill and inserted the forks under the rotors. He climbed off the tractor one more time and tied a 50-foot length of safety rope to the base of the tractor forks and the other end to the upper reaches of the trestle. Hopefully, this would keep the windmill from toppling over onto the truck. The thunder was rumbling, but Daddy never stopped mid-project.

"Get out of the way, Virginia." I ran over and jumped in the truck with Everett.

The forklift started to rise and with it the rusty, earth-encrusted head of the windmill. About three feet off the ground, Daddy started yelling some instructions we couldn't hear and wildly signaling us with a circular motion of his hand.

"What do you think he means?" Everett asked me.

"Looks like he wants us to get out and run around the truck."

Instead Everett turned on the winch at slow speed until all the slack was out of the cable, and Daddy gestured a big "yes" with his head and hands. Everett moved up one half point on my esteem scale. I could never comprehend Daddy's hand signals.

The upward motion continued from Daddy's end, and Everett kept the slack out of the cable until the forklift was as high as it could go. Daddy started with the wild circles again.

"I guess we're on our own now," Everett said. "What a way to die, a windmill vane through the brain." He pressed his hard hat tighter to his head and turned the winch back on.

As we pulled the windmill out of the Waldon's hands, Daddy slammed the tractor into reverse and drove straight back until all slack was out of the safety rope he had tied to the trestle and forks. I think he overestimated the length he would need, because he had to bump up over a few bushes and nearly break into the Benson house to get the rope taut. The wind had picked up and was working against us—crossways. Daddy was making faster circles with his hands and Everett turned the winch speed to high.

As we reeled in the cable, Daddy crept forward with the tractor trying to keep the slack out of his rope and lend some sideways stability against the wind. The windmill, still teetering on two back legs, hung in the balance point for a very long moment, Everett's eyes like pies against the truck windshield. Then the huge structure fell forward, the two front legs slamming into ground, the wood and metal shuddering as if it would fly apart. Everett and I both screamed. Daddy's rope was taut and shaking but it kept the windmill from continuing on over into the truck. The trestle wasn't quite vertical. One leg had missed its hole.

Daddy was not pleased. He came off the tractor with a purple face. I couldn't hear the words he was saying as he galumphed over to the trestle. Grabbing the aberrant wooden leg, he shook it like an angry bear. The windmill shuddered again, and the leg danced into the hole. He turned and flashed us a front-page grin. Lightning also flashed, followed quickly by thunder. Daddy did a fast hobble over to the truck and piled in with us.

The black cloud unleashed an intense hailstorm that clattered against the metal cab so loudly that we all clutched our hands over our ears. It lasted only ten minutes, and when it let up, a brilliant rainbow touched down in the desert right behind the old Benson house.

"Will you look at that rainbow." Daddy was jubilant. "I'm going for the pot of gold."

He sprang from the truck and headed for the Waldon that was still idling at the windmill. He detached the safety rope and drove the tractor over to where he had parked the utility bucket. Quickly re-attaching the bucket, he drove out into the desert. Everett and I watched him as he took a big bite out of the ground at the foot of the rainbow. He dumped the dirt in a pile and got off the tractor to examine it. Digging through it with his hands, he pulled out an enormous metal lid. He held it up toward our direction and waved it around. He searched out a stick in the pile and began beating on the lid like a cymbal to really get our attention. He seemed to have found at least the lid to the pot of gold.

"I wonder what my kid's going to turn out like," Everett said and sighed.

Failing to capture our interest, Daddy got back on the Waldon and dug with undampened enthusiasm. Everett pulled out his lunch box.

"Last night's pizza," he said as he unwrapped a package of aluminum foil. It turned out to be about a dozen freshly peeled green chilis. Wrong piece of foil. He moaned and put it away.

"Well at least I have a yogurt. I even remembered a spoon." He removed the lid of the strawberry-banana low-fat container and found a few leftover string beans. Cynthia never threw anything away. I thought he was going to start crying.

I pulled out the brown grocery bag I had stored behind the seat and set before Everett a luscious picnic. It was the thawed remains of the Baptism party—sausages and pastries—and a thermos of hot, very sweet coffee. He plowed into it like a starving man.

I began the clean-up work, detaching the winch cable from the windmill and collecting all the tools and leftover lumber into the back of the truck. I pulled debris out of the rusty metal tank that would hold the water pumped by the windmill. In case there were leaks, I planted a little packet of African daisy seeds around the perimeter. Finally, I hung a small pottery bell on a crossbar of the trestle.

Daddy kept digging. He had a hole about the size of a basement. Everett, in spite of the coffee, was sound asleep across the seat of the truck.

FROM THE JOURNAL OF HENRY DAVID TARANTULA

ROSE CANYON

I am like the proverbial back East storekeeper coming West to try to be a cowboy. The sun hits me, and it makes me crawl. My ascent of Rose Canyon was slow and painful as a prayer. Dizzy, I slam into shin daggers. My clothes are covered with burrs. My lungs have no capacity for elevation or steep climbing. This idea of metamorphosing into a rugged outdoorsman was born in an oxygen tent where I spent so much childhood as the damp intense Pennsylvania greenery knocked me with wave after wave of pneumonia, my sinuses, tonsils, bronchial tubes, alveoli always swollen and impacted with water. I was sensitive to every plant and animal and other child. Four years now in a desert climate have sucked my lungs dry, but mere ideas do not make skin into leather. And now, at the top of Rose Canyon, everything is red. Beige and gray and full of stickers on the way up, and now it's all red. The underbrush has lit up as the sun sinks. Even the small, scalloped leaves of scrub oak have taken on a redness. And the long fingers of the alder. I carve that outrageous word "red" into the trunk of an oak. I am exhausted and I lie beside a burning bush, a mountain maple with broad palmate leaves like hands, the sun dipping lower and the very air filled with ruby red rose. Why? Why should the mountain leaves turn glorious as they die? Why don't they just croak?

Chapter 27

THE TRACK OF THE WOLF

"The scale on which his studies proceeded was so large as to require longevity, and we were the less prepared for his sudden disappearance."
Ralph Waldo Emerson, *"Thoreau," The Atlantic, 1862*

I returned to school after spring break, the plaster track and Henry David's journal in my backpack, possessed by an intense energy.

After my Monday morning biology lecture on that first day back, I pushed my way down the auditorium aisle, going against the crowd of exiting students. My professor was still behind the podium packing his briefcase when I approached him with the track in my hand carefully wrapped in one of my father's white handkerchiefs.

"Dr. Rogers, I found a very unusual animal track in the desert near my home. I made a plaster cast of it and I wondered if you would take a look at it."

"Miss, my area of research is the effect of gamma rays and marigolds on the renal glands of male hamsters." Or something like that. "Now why would I want to look at an animal track?" He slammed his case closed and stalked off the stage without even looking me in the eye.

That first response was a shock, but I got more accustomed to it as I worked my way down the list of biology professors, never so much as unwrapping the track for one of them. I went to the Forest Service as well. I rode my bike to the downtown office, and the receptionist allowed me in to see the public information officer.

"Call me Fred," he said. He listened to my story, oohed over the plaster impression and paged a biologist.

"Where did you find this track?" The biologist seemed interested.

I was vague about the location. Instead I quizzed him, "Is this the track of a wolf?"

He was noncommittal. "It could be a coyote or even a wild dog. Wolves were pretty much eliminated from the southwestern United States by 1950. The population in Mexico has all but disappeared, too. There hasn't been a verified wolf sighting anywhere in this area for probably 35 years."

"But this track is too big to be a coyote or a dog."

"It depends on how old the track was and how soft the mud. Tracks tend to spread and will look bigger depending on time and conditions."

"But the details are so distinct. I don't think this track was very old."

"Frankly, the only way I can verify the existence of a wolf is to kill it and examine the skull."

"Are you telling me that you'd have to kill a wolf to prove it was alive? The only real wolf is a dead wolf?"

My grades soared from "A's to "A+"s in some sort of odd reverse rebellion. I compulsively attended to every detail of biology, chemistry, calculus, Latin, and English literature, even though they all seemed like dead languages. The language that was alive for me came from the journal of a dead man.

Without encroaching on any of my usual studies, I created a private cave for myself that I visited each morning, allowing myself three exquisite hours of work on the transcription of Henry David's cramped, backwards handwriting. His pages, sometimes mere scraps of paper, were filled to the very edges with scribbles and odd markings. I crept out of bed at four o'clock, tiptoeing in the dark trying not to wake my roommates. To make things easier, I slept in my clothes. I grabbed my backpack, prepared the night before with all the necessary materials, and slunk off to the main library which stayed open twenty-four hours.

On that very first early morning, the full moon sat on the western horizon, as yellow as a harvest moonrise, and I watched it drop behind the Tucson Mountains. Each subsequent morning it had waned by a sliver and traveled backwards one step toward the east. After a week it hung like a half-lantern at the zenith of the sky, brightly lighting my way to the library. In two weeks at four o'clock it was new, a thin white ring shining on the eastern horizon just above Mica Mountain. It was lit from below by the rising sun with Venus, the morning star, an arm's length away. And that was the last time I saw the moon until I went home to William, but the morning star stayed with me until the end of the semester.

The library was brightly lit and empty at four o'clock. Most students who burned the midnight oil did so at midnight. After the first couple of mornings, a security guard started bringing me an illegal cup of coffee from some back room. I promised him I'd be gone by seven when the day crew, who strictly adhered to the no food no drink rule, clocked in. He never tried to strike up a conversation and soon I was embroiled in the journal. The overhead lights seemed to focus to a spot on a page, and the library walls faded to gray. I often had to use the magnifying glass from the science kit to decipher a scrawled, spidery word, and I transcribed each one with clear penmanship into my special autumn leaf stamped notebook as if I were disentangling Henry David's matted hair with gentle fingers.

My own appearance became more and more disheveled, and my roommate Darla started to worry. She laid in wait for me one morning, which was the close of a particularly late evening for her. As I slipped out of bed, she slapped on the overhead light. The other roommates groaned and slammed pillows across their eyes though they were already covered with sleeping masks. Darla ignored their protests.

"Where are you sneaking off to in the middle of the night?" Four in the morning was the middle of the night to Darla.

"I'm going to meet a guy." I thought that would satisfy her, but she was still suspicious.

"This can't be true love or you'd be taking better care of yourself." She shoved me into the chair at her desk. Her desk had early on been converted to a make-up table with a large mirror as its centerpiece. The frame of the mirror was studded with light bulbs and she switched them on.

"Just look at yourself."

In the harsh light, I looked like a skeleton. I had lost weight and my eyes were ringed with black shadows.

"First off, you're going in the shower." She pulled the band off the end of my braid and started unweaving my hair. "And this time you are not shampooing with your braid still in." With her own hairbrush she brutally attacked my scalp and neglected, tangled tresses until they flowed along the soft waves created by the braid and flashed with electricity. She had me wailing.

"I don't believe in true love."

Then she tossed me her heavy white terrycloth bathrobe and ordered me into the bathroom.

The hot water was as magical as a good night's sleep, and when I returned to our room, the lights were off except for around the mirror. I could see that Darla's top dresser drawer was open and she called out from her bed, "At least take a pair of my underwear."

I took the leopard ones, put on clean sweats, and headed off to the library. As I quietly pulled the door closed, I heard Susan Jane mumbling.

"She is such a slut."

FROM THE JOURNAL OF HENRY DAVID TARANTULA

The outhouse in the Forest Service campground in Rose Canyon has the overwhelming smell of thick pink liquid disinfectant deodorizing soap. Until you lift the lid. Then the teeming swirling aroma of liquid shit hits like a punch in the face filling you with fear that you'll accidentally drop in your binoculars even though you don't have them with you. Fat flies buzz in and out between the slats. What if I get claustrophobia in there? I carve two letters above the door. PU. I opt for the open air.

Chapter 28

AMBUSH

"From where the sun now stands, I will fight no more forever!"
Chief Joseph, Nez Percé, *Surrender speech, Oct. 5, 1877*

In the cool of a May evening, a large white flower opened and hung rakishly upon the ancient, tattered saguaro that stood near the entrance of the cave where Henry David Tarantula had lived deliberately for a little more than one year. The plant, swollen with spring rains, made one last fling at immortality, producing the one blossom. A small black bat came buzzing and clicking in the night. It drank the nectar of the saguaro and fertilized the flower, though the plant would never live to bear another red fruit.

The next morning as the sun burned down on the desert foothills of the Santa Isabella Mountains, the flower closed and wilted, hanging like a sodden bonnet. Heat waves rose from the head of the saguaro and dozens of baby black widows ballooned off on silken threads.

On the Town Square in William, Mayor George P. Stone and his partner Howard Daugherty were at work before seven o'clock on the new Hardware. It rose from the ashes of the old store with a red antique brick face generously bespeckled with yellow-gold. George stopped work at ten o'clock to run home and change into his medium blue jacket for a television appearance. Today, true to his campaign promise, he had scheduled a clean-up of the desert caves. The media and the fire department had both been notified. Virginia had not been informed. George knew she would not approve ideologically, and he suspected she would think it a poor political move as well. Besides, she was so emotional lately, worse than Cynthia had ever been. Even Dot couldn't keep her under control on the phone. She was working on some crazy paper.

Shortly before noon, the desert east of William was bustling like a downtown parking lot. The press corps had arrived and was setting up cameras and stringing wires all around in the bushes. The Town Council had brought up a podium for George, which Dot had decorated with crepe paper flowers and the media with a multitude of microphones.

At precisely noon, George and Dot drove up in the bright blue International.

"I don't see the fire truck, Dot. What am I going to do if the fire truck doesn't get here?"

"Don't worry, Darling, it'll be here soon."

He waved and grinned at the reporters while trying to discretely gape back down the road in search of the firefighters. He made a U-turn near the cave and distractedly backed the International into the giant saguaro.

"Cheese 'n crackers." He yowled after making sure the windows were up. Then he got out of the truck smiling, opened the door for Dot and the two walked together to the podium. The uneven terrain was difficult for George to negotiate with no ankle motion, and he leaned heavily on his wife.

Cynthia and Everett were already in position. It was Baby Brick's first public appearance, and Cynthia had him ensconced in a broad brimmed baby blue bonnet. Everett had brought up a lawn chair for Cynthia, and the photographers were pressing close to her newly endowed chest in a sundress to snap pictures of the baby.

"Do you think he'll go into politics?" the morning *Star* asked Cynthia.

"He's going to be a chemist just like his father," Cynthia said, squeezing Everett's hand that rested possessively on her shoulder. Everett beamed. Brick's incredibly blue eyes were fixed on the camera and he flashed one of his giant toothless smiles.

George jumped into the act, speaking into the microphones. "I'd like to introduce the newest member of the Stone family, my grandson, Brick Palmer Stolz, born March 21. He's wearing a bonnet?"

Cynthia and Dot simultaneously glared at him.

"He's wearing a bonnet." He was decisive this time.

Now ready to begin his proclamation, George raised both hands over his head, but noticed that all the cameras were turned to a roadrunner who had just dashed onto the scene. The mixed-up frenzied bird ran one way, then another, grabbed a lizard, flashed its red eyelids at the Channel 4 News lens, then exited stage left. When that act was over and the cameras were finally paying attention to George, he once again raised his arms.

This time the wind intervened, producing a dust devil amid the reporters, wrenching their papers from their hands. So far, George wasn't having a good day. As the newsmen scrambled for their notes, the devil smacked the mayor, who was already unsteady, especially with his arms up. George did a full spin hollering his opening line, "It's summertime" before catching his balance with the podium.

On top of the battered saguaro—something George had not noticed in his rearview mirror when he slammed into it—sat a huge, burly, shiny, jet black raven. He had been as sullen as a statue all morning. On his shoulders, however, stood a slightly smaller and more active version of himself. She was constantly a-twitch, made small murmurings, and her head feathers were a mess. When the dust devil hit, the two ravens exited stage up.

George's composure was hanging by a shoelace until he spied the red fire truck making its painful way up the rocky road. A fire engine always perked him up.

"It's time, my friends, to go to war against the unkempt elements that have invaded our caves. They have tried to make fools of us with their irresponsible living, squatting and littering. We are here today to flush them out, literally flush them out. And here come the firefighters to do just that. In a few moments this desert will be returned to its original cleanliness, peace and integrity. I promised you this during my campaign, and it will be carried out."

"Sorry, Chief," said Fire Chief Bill Corti as he jumped out of the truck. "Hope we're not too late. We had a helluva time getting this engine up here. Got stuck in a sand wash."

The firefighters had brought the old red Engine 12, the Class A pumper, with five hundred gallons of water. Number 12 had been retired soon after George and was only used in training and parades. All of the new engines were green, a color George found abominable. Puke green, he called it, when Dot wasn't around.

"Glad to see you, boys." George was loud and jovial, but he whispered behind his hand to Corti, "Watch your language. Dot's here." Loudly again, "You're right on time. Now let's get to work."

His old crew had shown up, as loyal as ever. Lieutenant Lane—now Captain Lane—Brooks and Rodriguez. They didn't dare bring Emery. They still couldn't give him a radio let alone get him within ten miles of Dot. The four firefighters, in full yellow regalia despite the hot sun and no fire, unwound a two-and-a-half-inch hose and positioned themselves near the cave's entrance. What a photo opportunity. George took the nozzle with Corti right behind him, and the cameramen scurried to relocate their equipment for the shot.

"Stand back," George ordered the crowd. "Surround and drown," and he turned the water on.

It had been more than five years since George had commanded a fire hose, and the sexual relief was tremendous. He scoured the mouth of the cave making rainbows in the sunlight all around the entrance and pounded the dark interior with the writhing stream until dirty water poured back out. There was a commotion of metal as an air conditioner in pieces floated from the entrance, followed by a parade of aluminum beer cans.

Finally, George shut the water off. In the sudden silence there came from deep within the cave a loud, very human cough. The firemen pulled back toward their truck in surprise, but George stepped forward to face the unanticipated freeloader.

"Come on out into the light and see the music you slovenly son of a bee."

There was rustling among cans and a thrashing as if someone were shaking off a wet coat. A slow movement began toward daylight. All eyes, camera and otherwise, were glued to the entrance of the cave, but the mayor saw them first. Two disembodied yellow globes emerging from the dark.

"Cheese." It looked like a ghost.

Then came the beast himself. A black, disheveled, wet, three-legged...dog? He had the slow, sinewy movement of an asymmetrical dancer.

"Henry David?" George's voice was high-pitched. "Is that you?"

The animal continued forward toward the sour, salty-smelling mayor, halting about ten feet away.

"Dot...Dot...Do you think it's Henry David?" Dot, in a rare, inelegant move, had thrown her body across the baby.

"Shoot the bastard," she hissed.

Though his wet hair clung closely to his lean body, the mane of his neck bristled like a fringed ceremonial shirt, every hair standing on end, magnifying his stature. He vibrated with nervous, quick twitches like a tightly wound spring. His lips quivered upward exposing huge canines and a low, low growl rumbled from his enormous chest. He kept his head down, eyes on George's eyes, his whites visible below the yellow.

For George, it was like suddenly looking again into the soul of the hateful, fiery Hardware basement. He heard the roar of flames in his ears, sweat poured down his back, and his right leg throbbed. Canines probably can't distinguish Mediterranean blue, but the reflective color of George's eyes may have revealed the commonality of a metal foot. As the animal looked into George's eyes, maybe he saw himself. His right rear stump of a leg started shaking.

The press was motionless, their pens stopped mid-letter. Their catchy headlines: MAYOR STONEWALLED BY 3-LEGGED DOG and STONE'S CAMPAIGN PROMISE WASHES OUT, in their fingers. The only ones who screamed were the two ravens who had risen to the top of the swirling updraft of the dust devil.

"*Quork, quork, quork, quork, quork.*"

"*Eek, eek, eek.*"

They now began their descent plunging in a free fall, and it soon became apparent to those on the ground that the male was mounted on the female, and they were copulating mid-air.

"*Rrrock, rrrock, rrrock,*" croaked the male, and the two, still locked together, began a series of rolls and spins. Even the mayor and the black beast unlocked from each other's eyes to watch the show. To those who were counting, it was six somersaults and four half-twists.

"*Eddie,*" squealed the female raven. They descended straight into the crowd never checking their speed until they were almost head level. Then they careened sideways and landed down the hill in the black branches of a mostly dead pecan tree.

Dot held the bonnet brim over the baby's eyes. "That was disgusting," she said.

The black dog shook himself again, liberally spraying the mayor, turned and sauntered with a light step back into the cave, tail up.

Dot dashed across the rocks in her high heels, grabbed George by the arm and led him away from the cave and back into the family group.

"You don't think that was really Henry David, do you?" he asked her in a whisper.

"Of course not, Darling."

Everett spoke in a low tone. "George, I don't think that's a dog or a coyote. We've had rumors floating around at the mine for the past month about wolf sightings. Ranchers have been reporting losses. The feds have been looking into it and they think there may be a new migration from Mexico of the gray wolf. It's an endangered species, *Canis lupus baileyi.*"

George swept the faces of the reporters. His political sense told him he was about to go bust with the watermelon crop, and the cave clean-up did not look like it was going to revitalize his image. But he had seen something familiar in the eyes of the wolf. He moved to the podium with the same unswerving certainty he had when pulling Fireman Lane out of the burning Hardware roof.

"I hereby grant this injured animal sanctuary." The press snapped to attention. "What we have here is an endangered species—*Canis lupus*, uh, ballyhoo. I declare this area off limits to the public and the press until a full biological survey is completed." It could mean some professional work for Virginia.

Raising both arms in the air, he shouted, "Let this animal be."

The press was extremely happy to oblige. With nervous backwards glances over their shoulders toward the cave, they crammed equipment and uncoiled cords into their vans and blasted down the hill as if they were on deadline. The political tide had turned. George had started up a brass band in the brains of the media and headlines were already formulating for the wire. MAYOR STONE HEROICALLY SAVES SPECIES. Subhead: DOT SAYS SHOOT.

The wind had one final remark. It whirled into another dust devil and slammed into the old saguaro. It was a knock-out. After two hundred years of exposure to the elements and a solid punch from a pickup truck, the cactus gave up the ghost. Twenty thousand pounds of water, carefully stored during the winter rains, came careening down on the offending vehicle. The passenger's roof caved in and the windshield blew out.

"Spit house mouse" was George's loud response.

Dot turned toward Cynthia and rasped into her ear, "That cactus is Virginia. I know it. It's her right down to the soggy white hat."

George came wailing into Dot's arms.

"I've ruined my bright blue International."

"Don't worry, Darling, it can be fixed." Dot patted and cooed. "Let's catch a ride home in the fire truck."

FROM THE JOURNAL OF HENRY DAVID TARANTULA

I have been on the trail for three weeks, seeking my vision. My skin has gone from white to red to brown. I have nibbled on or smoked every greenish plant, boiled up or ground up every bean I could find, and swallowed ants, grasshoppers and beetles. I know my favorites. Up high I found berries. There is water at the top of every canyon, even at the broad, hot Bloomington Pass. My walls are falling away, the ceiling ever-changing. I wear fewer and fewer clothes. The light up here can be blinding.

This morning I woke up stiff as a grasshopper and staggering. A thin haze of cirrus was whipping across the sky throwing me off balance when I looked up. The valley below glared with dust. One hand over my eyes, I stumbled east and west. I knew the Window was there somewhere, slightly off the trail. I came upon it by surprise, tripped, and plunged into the hole. I sucked a deep breath and looked up, my eyes opened wide.

On the other side of the Window sat a jackrabbit the size of an antelope. Was it a jackalope? Did I see a mythical jackalope? What is its significance? He waved his ears at me, and I reeled backwards out of the Window and into the dirt. I bolted upright again and jumped through the window, like a jackrabbit myself. This time I saw a small rabbit taking off into the bushes. I beat around in the creosote, calling the jackalope. Here Jack, poopoopeedoo. What I found was a battered pair of motorcycle goggles. I knew I had achieved the fruit of my quest. These goggles, the gift of the jackalope, will give me vision and protect me from the elements. I climbed back into the Window, wearing the goggles, and played my harmonica, "Proud Mary," Credence Clearwater Revival.

Chapter 29

THE GIFT

"I do not see how he can ever die; Nature cannot spare him."
Henry David Thoreau, *Walden*

Daddy came into the dormitory lobby to pick me up at the end of the semester.

"Do I look any different?" I quizzed him and he immediately started to squirm. He knew no woman, especially Dot, wanted a wrong answer to that question.

"Um, a new dress?" And there was no man worse than Daddy in answering that question, which was part of the fun in asking.

"Daddy, I'm wearing jeans. Didn't you notice I cut my hair?" Right up to the ears. Without the sanction of braids and rubber bands, my hair had a crazy, curling mind of its own.

"Oh, yes." He was beaming now that he had figured out the right answer. "You look like my little Ginny Loo-Who again."

"It's supposed to make me look more grown-up."

"Come on outside, Ginny Loo-Who, I've got something new to show *you*, too."

He picked up my big suitcase, I grabbed the bike that was parked right outside the door, and we headed for the parking lot.

"How do you like my new Toyota? It gets great gas mileage."

The truck was small, white and nondescript even though it had the old winch on the front and the old toolbox in the back. My arms and legs went stiff.

"Where's the bright blue International?"

"I put a few dents in it and busted out the windshield. I decided it was time for a new truck. You'll love the way this thing rides."

I didn't make a move to help him load my things into the shiny white bed. "You've wrecked the bright blue International?" My face and voice were pretty stiff, too.

"Of course not. That truck is too tough to be totaled. I just had a minor run-in with a cactus. Did you know that a full-blown saguaro can weigh up to ten tons? The guy who fixed the truck couldn't believe it either when he was pounding out all the dents. New glass, new paint, she looks like new."

He stopped packing the Toyota and reached into his pocket. "Oh, here's the keys." It was the same old ring with the worn-out St. Christopher medal on it. He tossed it to me. "It's all yours. I thought you might be needing it for your science projects."

I almost knocked him over with my hug, and I didn't mention that I had changed my major to art. He would have understood that less than biology.

"Daddy, your new truck is just beautiful. I can't wait to ride in it."

I think my father's present of the bright blue International was his way of trying to pull me out of the clouds—where I had been roosting for the past two months—and back into the material world.

Daddy jabbered all the way home in the Toyota, though he didn't mention the clean-up of the caves. I got all those details from Cynthia later. He said the Hardware had reopened for business though it was now called Daugherty's and sold fine china. Louise Daugherty ran the show and he and Howard were silent partners, with Louise placing a strong emphasis on the "silent." He had a new collection of "antique" bricks which he got from tearing down the old William water tower, and he felt it only appropriate to build something out of brick for Brick.

I finally got in one question. "Is the windmill pumping water?"

"No problemo. Rodriguez—you remember Fireman Rodriguez, don't you?—welded the pipe back together, and the whole doom-a-phlage couldn't wait to get back to work. It still squeaks a little."

As we were pulling into William, he mentioned that a big animal had been spotted in the Santa Isabella foothills that Everett thought was a Mexican wolf, an endangered species. My stomach jumped.

"*Canus lupus ballyhoo.* As mayor I called for a biological study. The Forest Service came in on off-road vehicles like a bunch of knuckleheads. They drove up and down the canyons howling. Never found spit. They're saying we've imagined it. Cheese, Channel 4 has the farking thing on film."

I asked Daddy, "Have they given up the search?"

"Unless we come up with further evidence like tracks or howling or kills, they're writing it off."

I had plenty of evidence in my day pack—the plaster cast of the wolf track. I also carried Henry David's journal and my own transcription, like the track of Henry David's gnarled hand. I kept the pack close to me up front in the cab. If the wolf had left the Santa Isabella Caves, I knew someplace else he would like to hang out.

"After that experience, I doubt if anyone will report anything," Daddy said. "We don't want the feds breathing down our necks. I said right from the very beginning, we should leave the animal alone. Leave the desert to the desert creatures."

"Daddy, are you becoming an environmentalist?"

He took a mock swing at me.

Daddy's efforts to keep me out of the clouds were, of course, futile, but at the same time I loved the feel of my hands on the steering wheel and feet on the stubborn pedals of the old truck. Before I unpacked a thing, I drove out to the Old Benson place. The entire sky was painted with big curling white cirrus feathers. The windmill was upright, solid and turning. The rusty metal tank was holding water. The desert had undergone a subtle change.

As the breeze came up in the afternoon, the creaking of the windmill and the tiny tinkling of my pottery bell had become as familiar as the midday silence, the call of mourning doves, and the clatter of empty cans rolling down the road. The tank was a new focal point with its magnetizing smell of sweet water. African daisies sprang up and butterflies pollinated. Birds came for their baths. A lost cow found protection there and sometimes sulked beneath the tower. The coyotes praised God. A few secretive deer came down from the mountain.

All summer vacation I visited the Benson place early every morning, recording in my field notebook the presence of the cow, deer, coyotes, skunks, ground squirrels, rabbits, quail, mice, doves, sparrows, ravens and javelina. I saw birds and rabbits and the cow during those daytime visits, but the others had come secretly in the dark or dawn, chronicling their adventures in the soft mud around the leaky water tank. I began to read their dainty prints and messy scrawls with the same certainty that I transcribed Henry David's journal.

I had found no naturalists in the biology department at the University of Arizona. My professors' views of biology did not venture beyond a laboratory Petri dish. Most of my fellow students were pre-med and murderously competitive, willing to cheat to get the highest grade on a test. I chose to study biology in the art department.

"Thought any more about going into politics, Virginia?" Daddy hadn't given up. I answered him with only a low laugh, for what is art if not anarchy?

I set up my easel at the Benson place and resurrected Martha's gardens on canvas. I started with the roses, imagining their aroma, painting long rows, each row a different shade of yellow, pink, red and purple. I straightened her twisted house, added a coat of thick white paint, and put on a new roof of expensive mission tile. I painted sweet peas up the south wall in mixed colors, lots of blues. I copied the windmill just as it now really stood, including the small bell, extrapolating only a thin vine of honeysuckle climbing up the trestle.

In the forefront of the picture, I reconstructed the mailbox, labeled BENSON, and nearly buried it in a bush of purple and white foxglove. I planted pecan trees for shade in the front yard and at their feet I had African daisies sprouting. Above the house the top of a huge cottonwood growing beside Cholla Creek was half-lit with yellow-green spring leaves. I put in some buttercups along the walkway, and a small, narrow field of white carnations adjacent to the roses.

I waited for the wolf to feel the power of my gift. I imagined that he woke up facing in this direction, his wanderings becoming slightly weighted toward it. A curiosity must be kindling in him as to what lay among these cholla-covered hills. Finally, he'd be drawn like a willow to the water. I studied my painting, deciding where to put the last detail. Amid the roses? Carnations? Finally, in the cluster of foxglove at the mailbox I painted two pointy black ears.

Why was Bruce Smith called The Snake? I began to ponder this question. Henry David had warned me the last night I saw him that Bruce was a snake. Did he speak with a forked tongue? Was there some remote chance that Bruce had manufactured Henry David's demise to stamp out the competition for my affection? Why hadn't Mom seen a death notice? She reads three newspapers every Sunday—William, Tucson and Phoenix. She always turns to the obituaries first. Surely Daddy would have told her Henry David's real name.

How does one verify a death or a life? With the presence of a skull? Did I need to know for sure that the wolf lived or that Henry David died? Better to let the wolf live without verification and Henry David die without absolute certainty. With each there is the hope of sudden appearance.

In the afternoons, I work on the ceiling of Brick's nursery. Mom will never forgive Cynthia for loving the clouds and cerulean blue of my bedroom and asking me to paint clouds for Brick. Brick is a born politician, his hands always in the air, commanding a constant entourage of doting followers.

At night I close my eyes and can still see the Gila River. The wind is quiet, the blinding sun has at last disappeared, and I float in my bed watching the dark water.

When I awake in the morning, I scan the clouds on my ceiling, then carefully read over the vibrant patterns on the pine walls of my bedroom. I can clearly see Henry David's hand in the paneling, palm-out, lined with concentric circles, a knot in the center like a wound. I see arms and legs curled like limber branches, and unmistakably his face, his eyes and mouth dark holes, his spidery hair crawling through the intricate pattern of the wood.

Epilogue

FROM THE JOURNAL OF VIRGINIA STONE SAGUARO

DANCE OF THE CACTI
How does one speak to a cactus? Especially after twenty-five years.

Saguaro,

Your name itself like wind moaning through needles, this mountain a sanctuary, the hillside forested with oblates, arms raised worshipping the sky, light glaring through a gauze of clouds. I have learned that you are probably all dead—from drought and frost. Yet you still stand, creeping infinitesimally toward falling, dying as slowly as living— thirty years to become a toddler, fifty to flower, seventy-five for the first arm, what can I say, standing still, reminding?

The Forest Service has constructed a broad trail through the once remote Santa Isabella foothills and then up Rose Canyon, complete with water bars and even stair steps in places. "Stay on the Trail," signs say everywhere, and people do. They don't know where else to go with no memories and many fears. One saguaro, pockmarked, leans slightly toward passersby, two branches curving upward like the arms of a candelabrum. I lean also, in conversation, arms up like candles. A hiker steams past, ignoring us both, tunes wired into her ears, floppy straw hat, oversized sunglasses, black tights extending just below her knees, black T-shirt depicting in glitter the planets of the solar system, French cut, salmon-colored, polka-dotted leotard peeking out, philosophically, what do I know? Down in the city, the underground aquifer is drained dry, the whole valley settling into the gap, brick walls cracking, people now drinking foul-smelling river water.

More people are swarming down the trail, like a craze of ants but unable to keep quiet. I duck into the desert following my old path by instinct. Climbing uphill through the microscopic buzzing of pollen, insects twittering, I find an age-old disciple with rotted head, all its branches broken, but it has a clump of new growth from its waist like lots of little babies with open arms popping out of its pocket. I, too, am slow growing, my hands are in my pockets. Have you seen any doves? Flying in gray curtains to maize fields at dawn? Maize has been converted to cotton, then abandoned to thistle as the city buys land for water rights, know what I'm saying, mourning?

Attention, a single stump, no taller than me, no branches. It should be young, but its accordion skin is mottled with scabs and holes. I stand erect speaking into the black bacterial necrotic face, have you noticed? People have exchanged thin lacy café curtains for full-length drapes that don't even open behind iron bars. Crime multiplies like sewer roaches, people keeping their drains closed at night or something disgusting might crawl out of the bathroom, what can I do, ever, thin-skinned, susceptible?

Cholla, with your huge head of hair full of static and fruit. Ocotillo, I'm swaying with you from the hips, a tiny breeze causing so much emotion in my fingers. Saguaro, with five arms all twisted around your body, I'm spinning too, almost crashing into your sister, two new arms sprouting from her center. I likewise lock my upper arms to my torso, converse with her in sign language, gesturing from my waist how I long for rain. Another saguaro has only one arm remaining and even that is rotting at the base, but it is held very high like an old mother waving. And so I look up, feel my hair flowing down my back, and I reach, my eyes following my own wavering arm toward sky.

Why, after twenty-five years, is it your arms, your faces that I draw in my notebook at night, your gray-green that I find endlessly fascinating, your one-day-only white blooms that satisfy me for a full year? Why would anyone ever want to dance with a cactus or hug a tree?

I arrive at the dark-trunked, ancient pecan, its feet still buried in the arroyo whose infrequent flows have failed to inspire new life. Light ricochets off the limestone walls above. I can still read that old remark on the tree, "Clem." There is another message, too, carved long ago and healed over, "I love you forever."

Acknowledgments

This book has experienced a very long infancy. It started with a poem when I was eighteen years old on my first desert cook-out with my friend Cheryl and her sister Adrienne. Poetry revisions carried me through college and evolved into a short story, then two, then became the rudimentary start of a novel. I carried Henry David Tarantula with me when I moved from Arizona to Wyoming, and Wyoming people seemed to appreciate him. An early chapter was published in the *Casper Star-Tribune Arts Section* in 1984, and I was awarded the Wyoming Arts Council's Frank Nelson Doubleday Award for a Woman Writer (for short fiction) in 1988. Gosh, we're still back almost 40 years ago!

My sister Susan discovered a Tucson artist Kathleen Stoll, whose paintings of Southwestern scenes intrigued her, and I thought the style would be perfect for my envisioned novel. On a wild hair (or was it a wild hare as in magic jackrabbit?), we went to visit the artist. She welcomed us at her Tucson ranch, and I gave her a copy of my chapter, telling her of my hope that she might illustrate my (soon-to-be-finished) novel. (Ha! This is in the 1980s.) After reading my selection, Kathy painted me a picture, which now graces the cover. This past year, after 40 years, Kathy was still on the ranch, remembered me and gave her permission. A crazy miracle!

Now to finish the book. While working as Director of the Teton County Library in Jackson, Wyoming, I took a community college class "Write Your Novel." It was taught by amazing novelist Tim Sandlin. If I remember correctly, the horrifying assignment was to write for four hours a day. The most I could give was two hours, which I could only find between 4:00 and 6:00 a.m. It did get me to the first very short but entire draft. Again, this skimpy draft was put on hold for about ten years as I went to law school. After practicing for seven years, my triplet grandchildren were born, and I dropped everything and headed for Portland, Oregon. My unbelievably strong and capable daughter sent me, my husband, and the other grandparents back home after three months. Jobless, I had a marvelous dream in which a very handsome, warm, loving gentleman (It could *not* have been Henry David!) asked me, "What about all those books you wanted to write?"

I was back at it, and here I am now after another nine years. Hooray!

Grateful acknowledgment goes to the following institutions, which granted me permission to use excerpts from their publications:

Casper Star-Tribune Arts Section, July 22, 1984, p. 12, "Henry David Tarantula Hips for Mayor" (an early version of Chapter 1).

The Museum of Northern Arizona Press for epigraphs excerpted from The Tohono O'odham Mockingbird and Seating Speeches in *Rainhouse and Ocean: Speeches for the Papago Year* by Ruth M. Underhill, Donald M. Bahr, Baptisto Lopez, Jose Pancho, and David Lopez. Vol. 4 (American Tribal Religions), a monograph series, Karl W Luckert, General Editor, published by The Museum of Northern Arizona Press, 1979.

All other epigraphs are in the public domain.

I would like to thank the Wyoming Arts Council, *Casper Star-Tribune,* and Tim Sandlin for their support along the way. Participants in the Masters Workshop at the Tucson Festival of Books contributed helpful critique. Thanks also to Wyoming Writers, Inc. for their efforts to bring national publishers to Wyoming. It was that group's conference that connected me with Winter Goose's Jessica Kristie, whose careful editing and persistence have brought this long effort to happy fruition.

I'm still in loving shock over the talent, memory, and generosity of Tucson artist Kathleen Stoll. Thank you, Kathy! Cheers to Fireman Jim Loose for walking me through an imaginary fire and to Katsey Long for instructing me on painting a ceiling. My husband Joe taught me desert plants, birds and rocks and guided me up most every canyon and peak in Southern Arizona, thereby changing my life.

Forever love to my husband and brilliant writer daughter Eve, who have encouraged my writing all these years.

About the Author

Betsy Orient Bernfeld is a writer, librarian, and lawyer in Jackson Hole, Wyoming. Originally from Tucson, Arizona, Betsy grew up hiking and backpacking in the territory ambience of Edward Abbey's monkeywrench gang.

The humorous environmental love story *The Journal of Henry David Tarantula* is Betsy's first novel. It received early acclaim on the 2016 Short List of the Santa Fe Writer's Project and as a finalist in the 2017 New Rivers Many Voices Project. Recipient of the 2020 Wyoming Arts Council's Creative Writing Fellowship for Poetry, Betsy is author of two poetry collections, *Eve* and *The Cathedral Is Burning*.

Betsy lives with her husband Joe and their black lab Magnolia in a little log cabin at the base of the Grand Teton Mountains.

www.ingramcontent.com/pod-product-compliance
Lightning Source LLC
Chambersburg PA
CBHW031237260626
47169CB00007B/2343